Rebecca's Family and Friends

Papa
Rebecca's father, who
owns a small shoe store

Mama
Rebecca's mother, who
keeps a good Jewish home

Sadie and Sophie
Rebecca's twin sisters,
who are fourteen

Benny and Victor
Rebecca's brothers, who
are five and twelve

Max
Mama's cousin,
a professional actor

Grandpa
Rebecca's grandfather,
a Russian immigrant

Bubbie
Rebecca's grandmother,
a Russian immigrant

The Sound of Applause

by Jacqueline Dembar Greene

★ American Girl®

A Peek into
Rebecca's World

Rebecca's stories take place in the Lower East Side of Manhattan, in New York City. In 1914, this was a busy, crowded neighborhood full of immigrants from Russia, Italy, and many other parts of Europe.

Uncle Jacob
Ana's father, who brings his family over from Russia

Aunt Fannie
Ana's mother, who wants a better life for her family

Ana
Rebecca's nine-year-old cousin from Russia

Josef and Michael
Rebecca's cousins, who are fifteen and thirteen

Rose
A girl in Rebecca's class who immigrated a while ago

Leo Berg
A conceited boy from Rebecca's class

Mrs. Berg
Leo's mother, who wants nothing but the best

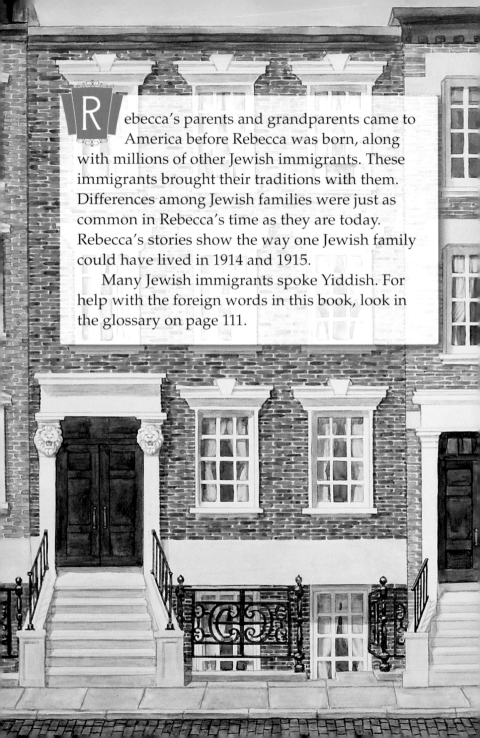

R ebecca's parents and grandparents came to America before Rebecca was born, along with millions of other Jewish immigrants. These immigrants brought their traditions with them. Differences among Jewish families were just as common in Rebecca's time as they are today. Rebecca's stories show the way one Jewish family could have lived in 1914 and 1915.

Many Jewish immigrants spoke Yiddish. For help with the foreign words in this book, look in the glossary on page 111.

Table
of Contents

A Sabbath Surprise

Rebecca Rubin tugged at her wooden doll until the top and bottom pulled apart to reveal a smaller doll nesting inside. There were seven painted dolls in all, each one tucked inside the next. They reminded Rebecca of her family, which numbered exactly seven.

The dolls had belonged to Mama when she was growing up in Russia, before Rebecca was born. But now the Russian dolls were Rebecca's treasure. She lined them up along the parlor windowsill, behind the sheer curtains.

"Ladies and gentlemen, your attention please!" said Rebecca to her imaginary audience. Slowly she drew back the curtains and wiggled the doll she thought of as the mother to the front of the windowsill stage.

"It's almost sundown," Rebecca said in a no-nonsense mama voice. "I hope you've all had your baths." She moved the mama closer to one of the smaller dolls. "Beckie, dear," she said sweetly, "you are so grown-up now. Tonight *you* may light the candles."

Rebecca pretended two of the bigger dolls were her older sisters. She moved them to face the mama and squawked in a high voice, "She's not old enough! She's practically a baby!" The two big-sister dolls butted into the little Beckie doll, and it wobbled close to the edge of the windowsill.

Rebecca pushed the papa doll until it stood in front of the others. "Well, curl my mustache," she said in a deep voice. "Beckie's not a baby anymore. She knows the Hebrew blessing perfectly. She is certainly old enough to light the candles tonight."

Before Rebecca could make her brother dolls speak, Mama's very real voice broke into her performance.

"Beckie, you'll have to put away your dolls," she called from the kitchen. "It's time to set the table."

"Phooey!" Rebecca said under her breath. She let the curtains fall across her dolls and turned back to the parlor. Extra leaves had been placed in the table to make room for everyone, and Rebecca smoothed the large white table-cloth. She set out two silver candlesticks and placed one white candle in each.

Every Friday, Mama cooked and cleaned all day to prepare for the Sabbath. *Bubbie*, Rebecca's grandmother, came down from her apartment upstairs to help cook. Before the sun set, the family came together for a special dinner. Friday night was Rebecca's favorite time of the week. *But Mama should let me do something more important than just setting the table,* she thought as she lifted a tall stack of Mama's best dishes from the sideboard.

Mama looked in from the kitchen. "Don't carry too many plates at once!" she cautioned. "And we need one extra tonight."

"Who's coming?" Rebecca asked, adding a plate to the stack. Through the doorway, she could see Bubbie frying fish in a black iron pan. Mama and Bubbie glanced at each other, but Mama did not answer Rebecca's question.

That made Rebecca even more curious to know who would be sharing their Sabbath dinner. "Who is it, Mama?"

Mama stirred sizzling potatoes and onions as she answered. "My cousin, Moyshe."

Now Rebecca nearly did drop the plates. "The actor?" she asked. She had overheard her parents talking about Moyshe before, but she had never met him. He usually traveled around the country, acting in vaudeville shows, but other times he was out of work and needed to borrow money from Papa. Rebecca had always wondered what an actor was like in real life, when he wasn't onstage. Tonight she would find out.

Rebecca took special care setting the table. She folded the linen napkins so that the crocheted edges were lined up neatly. If a real actor was coming to dinner, she wanted everything to be perfect.

"Sadie! Sophie!" Bubbie called. A few strands of gray hair slipped from her neat bun and framed her round face. She opened the oven door and slid out two braided loaves of *hallah* bread. Bubbie only baked hallah for Friday nights and holidays. Each loaf needed two eggs, and eggs were expensive.

Rebecca's twin sisters hurried in, wearing matching dresses. Sadie's eyes sparkled, and she looked eager to help. Sophie followed behind her.

"Come check if hallah is done," Bubbie instructed them.

"But the loaves are so hot," Sophie complained. She pulled away from the open oven. Sadie wasn't timid at all. She rapped two fingers against the shiny crust. A hollow sound echoed back.

"Done," Sadie announced.

Why doesn't Bubbie ever ask me to check the bread? Rebecca wondered. *Bubbie treats me like a little child!* She pushed past her sisters.

"I can do it, too," she said.

"So, give a tap," Bubbie told her. "When dough is done, bread sounds empty."

As Rebecca knocked on the bread with her knuckles, her older brother, Victor, sneaked up and rapped on her head. "Done!" he teased. The twins giggled.

Rebecca tried to swat Victor's arm, but before she could

catch him, a rhythmic knock sounded at the kitchen door.
Everyone turned to stare as it creaked open. A tall young
man wearing a jaunty straw hat and holding a polished
cane poked his head into the room.

"Moyshe!" Mama exclaimed.

The man put his finger to his lips, signaling everyone
to be quiet, and began sprinkling something in the doorway. Rebecca couldn't see anything in his hand. Her little
brother, Benny, squatted down. He looked at the floor, and
then up at Moyshe.

"What you are putting on this clean floor?" Bubbie
cried.

Moyshe peered into the hallway and looked around
nervously. Then he made more frantic sprinkling motions.
Finally, he spoke. "It's lion powder," he said solemnly.

Rebecca frowned. "What in the world is that?"

"Why, don't you know?" Moyshe asked. "It keeps the
lions away."

Benny's eyes grew wide. "Lions?"

Sadie sniffed. "That's ridiculous. There aren't any lions
around here."

"You see how well it works!" Moyshe announced.

Benny heaved a sigh of relief. Sadie and Sophie shook
their heads at the silly joke. Rebecca burst out laughing.

Moyshe flashed a gleaming smile. "At least one person

in this audience likes my joke," he said. "If you make them laugh, your audience will love you." He winked at Rebecca. "Remember that!"

Rebecca had never imagined that Mama's cousin would be so exciting. He even looked interesting, with his bright, dark eyes and the cane draped over his arm.

"Come in and close the door, Moyshe," Mama said.

"Excuse me, but it's no more Moyshe Shereshevsky," her cousin said. "I am Max Shepard, if you please." He gave a low bow, sweeping his hat off his head. "An American name for an American actor."

"America," Bubbie grumbled. "Always changing with the names. You don't change a name like a dirty shirt!"

Max didn't argue. "You must be little Beckie," he said, giving Rebecca his full attention. "You were toddling around like a windup doll the last time I saw you. Now you're a young lady!"

Rebecca beamed. Visitors never talked to her first when they met the family—they always fussed over Sadie and Sophie because they thought twins were so remarkable. If only they knew how left out Rebecca felt, being their younger sister!

Max turned to Benny. "And you weren't even born! Now you're old enough to grow buttons."

"Buttons don't grow!" Benny said.

Max pulled something from Benny's ear. "This sure looks like a button to me."

Benny's eyes grew wide as Max dropped a shiny brown button into his hand. Rebecca chuckled. How did Max do it?

"And this must be the *bar mitzvah* boy!" Max exclaimed, shaking Victor's hand. "Your mother tells me you're almost thirteen now, and studying hard for your bar mitzvah." He dropped his voice lower, as if sharing a secret. "But I hear sneaking out to play baseball is a lot more fun than studying Hebrew." Victor grinned.

"Good *Shabbos*!" Rebecca's grandfather called as he and Papa came in. Grandpa and Bubbie often mixed Yiddish words with their English. Yiddish was the language most Jewish immigrants in the neighborhood spoke. Rebecca could speak it, too, and she knew Shabbos meant Sabbath.

Papa handed Mama a penny bouquet of flowers, as he did every Friday. "Almost as pretty as you," he smiled. Mama blushed at the compliment as she hung her apron on a nail by the stove.

"Good evening, Moyshe," Papa said, shaking hands.

"Excuse me, but that's Max," Bubbie corrected him. "There is no more Moyshe."

Max grinned. "Moyshe, Max, what's the difference?

You can call me anything, as long as you don't call me late for dinner!"

Rebecca thought Max was funny. He was nothing like Papa, who was usually so serious.

"Such a busy day at the shoe store," Grandpa said. "But now it's Shabbos, and time to rest."

pushke

Papa took the *pushke*, the tin charity box, from the kitchen shelf. Every Friday night he put in his loose change. When the box was full, Papa brought the money to the synagogue. The congregation used the funds they collected to help new immigrants.

Papa dropped in the coins from his pocket, and they clanged to the bottom.

Grandpa added some change. "We must always help those who are less fortunate," he said. He held the box out to Max, but just at that moment Max stepped into the parlor and started tickling Benny until the boy was screaming with laughter.

"Don't make him wild," Mama scolded. "Come, it's time to light the candles."

Benny dashed to Papa and pulled at his sleeve. "My turn! My turn!"

Papa lifted Benny in the air, and Benny squealed with delight. "Women light the Shabbos candles," Papa said.

"No fair!" Benny whined.

"Can't I light them tonight?" Rebecca begged. "I know the prayer by heart."

"You heard Papa," Sadie said. "It's for the women in the family."

Rebecca frowned. This was just like her windowsill play!

"The twins will light the candles," Mama said firmly. "After all, they're fourteen."

"And not married yet?" Max joked. "Time to call the matchmaker!" The twins put their hands over their mouths to stifle their giggles.

Rebecca went to the windowsill and poked the big-sister dolls so hard, they rocked a little. "When will I get to light the candles?" she muttered. "The twins get to do *everything*!"

"Stop pouting and help," Bubbie ordered. She set a soup tureen on the sideboard and ladled golden chicken soup into bowls. Rebecca served Max first. He closed his eyes and breathed deeply, as if smelling a sweet perfume.

The family waited while Bubbie hung her apron in the kitchen. Then she sat down and straightened the lacquer pin she often wore. It was a keepsake she had brought with her from Russia. Rebecca had always loved the picture of the leaping hare that was painted on the pin's shiny black background. The picture was from a Russian folktale called Clever Karina. Sadie and Sophie stood before the silver candlesticks. Everyone watched as they lit the white candles with a long wooden match. Then they closed their eyes and recited the Hebrew prayer together, giving thanks for the Sabbath, a day of rest and peace. The candles flickered, lighting up the twins' faces with a golden glow.

"Beautiful," Max murmured. The grown-ups nodded approvingly, and Rebecca felt a bubble of envy grow in her chest. She was old enough to do more than just set the table!

Victor raised the special cup of Sabbath wine and recited the Hebrew blessing. Grandpa corrected his pronunciation, and Rebecca felt secretly pleased. Next, Mama removed the delicately embroidered hallah cover from the warm bread. She held up the two loaves, and the whole family gave thanks for their food. Rebecca said the prayer loudly so that everyone would know she didn't make mistakes.

Rebecca sipped her steaming soup, with Mama's homemade noodles. She loved the foods that made Friday nights special. But tonight she wasn't thinking about dinner. An idea was flickering in her mind, forming a glow as bright as the Sabbath candles.

A Showy Dinner

Mama set platters of food on the table, and Max spooned out a big helping of potatoes. "There's a new play coming to the Yiddish theater," he announced.

"Such a long time it's been since we see a play!" Grandpa said.

"We don't want to see Yiddish plays," Sadie said. "We like moving pictures." As usual, Sophie didn't say a word, but she nodded in agreement.

"Moving pitch-es," Grandpa said in his thick accent. "Why you want to see people moving in pitch-es when you can see real people moving onstage?"

"Movies are smooth," Sophie said. "We're going to see a show tomorrow with our friends."

Grandpa seemed puzzled. "What is this *smooth*?"

"It means modern and exciting!" said Sadie.

Rebecca could only imagine what a moving picture looked like. She had seen posters advertising the newest movies, but she had never been to one. "Can I come?" she asked.

The twins stopped their spoons in midair. With one

voice they replied, "You're not old enough."

"You always leave me out," Rebecca argued.

"We're in high school," Sadie reminded her, as if Rebecca hadn't heard that a thousand times.

"There's plenty of time for that nonsense when you're older," Papa declared. "I don't think these new moving pictures are meant for children."

Rebecca fumed. The twins got to do everything together. Even at night, they whispered under their covers while her bed stood alone on the opposite side of the room.

Victor glanced at Grandpa with an impish grin and then turned to Benny. "Speaking of pitch-es," he said to his brother, "how about catching baseballs for me tomorrow afternoon?"

Benny wiggled with excitement. "I can get the ball even if it rolls under the fence!"

The twins are best friends, and Victor and Benny can play ball together, Rebecca thought, *but I have only myself. I'm always left out, even on Friday nights.*

Rebecca thought of her friend Rose. She had her own candlesticks and lit the candles beside her mother every Sabbath. *If I had some candlesticks of my own,* Rebecca thought, *Mama would have to let me light candles.* Her idea began to glow more brightly. She could stand right next to Sadie and Sophie. Then they'd see she was old enough to perform the ceremony, and even old enough to go to the movies!

"I heard the Boston Red Sox have a new player," Max said, taking two crispy pieces of fish. "His name's Babe Ruth."

"Babe?" Bubbie scowled. "This is a name?"

"I read about him in the paper," Victor said. "They say he's going to be an ace pitcher. I wish he was playing for the Yankees."

"If he's good," Max said, "maybe we'll sign him next year."

"Enough about baseball," Papa said. "Now that school has started, I want to hear how my children are doing."

"In English class, we're reading a wonderful play called *Hamlet*," Sadie announced.

"It's by William Shakespeare," Sophie added softly.

Max looked pleased. "Ahh—the very best of theater."

Rebecca butted in. Why should her sisters get all the attention? "I got one hundred and ten percent on my arithmetic test," she announced, looking directly at Papa. "Miss Maloney gave us an extra credit problem, and I even got that right."

"Doing well in school is indeed something to be proud of," Mama said gently, "but be careful not to boast." She wagged her finger at the children. "You don't realize how lucky you are. In Russia, we never had the chance to go to school."

Max nodded in agreement. "Life was hard growing up in Russia. But I have fond memories, too." He lightly touched Bubbie's pin with the picture of the leaping hare. "I remember my mother telling me the story of Clever Karina."

Rebecca knew the story well, because Mama had often told it at bedtime. Max began telling the tale, his deep voice as silky as a singer crooning a tune.

"One morning, a poor farmer was overjoyed to see his horse had given birth to a foal. It was sleeping under a hay wagon in his neighbor's field. The farmer's wealthy neighbor said, 'Everyone knows a newborn rests beneath its mother. Since my hay wagon is obviously the mother, that handsome foal is mine.'"

"That's a-diculous!" Benny declared, and everyone chuckled.

Max went on, telling how the poor man told his only child, Karina, what had happened. Rebecca was drawn into the story. She imagined she was little Karina, trying to help. Acting the role, she said in a sweet voice, "Go to the *tsar*, Father, and ask him to settle the matter."

Max gave Rebecca a broad smile. He reached for Mama's flowered shawl and draped it around Rebecca's head. Now she truly felt as if she was in a play, acting the role of Karina.

Max continued. "But when the tsar heard the story, he did not make a decision. Instead he posed a riddle. The tsar said to the two men, 'You must each bring your youngest daughter to me, but she must not come on foot nor on horseback. She must not wear clothes, but she must not be naked. She must not bring a present, but she must come with a gift. The one who solves my riddle will keep the foal.'"

"Phooey on the tsar!" Grandpa scoffed.

"The poor farmer trudged home," said Max, "and told his daughter of the impossible riddle. But Clever Karina knew just what to do."

Rebecca acted out Karina's solution as Max told the end of the tale. "So Karina wrapped herself in her father's fishnet and rode off to the tsar's palace on the back of a giant hare. In her hand she carried a partridge in a cage. When she arrived before the tsar, Karina held up the birdcage."

Rebecca lifted her hand, looking determined. "Here is a gift, Your Majesty," she said, and she pretended to open a latch on a cage. Her hands made a graceful flapping motion, as if a bird were flying away.

"The tsar was pleased with Karina's clever solution to his riddle and decreed that her father should keep the foal.

*Rebecca pretended to open a latch on a cage. Her hands made
a graceful flapping motion, as if a bird were flying away.*

〜ᑐ **16** ᑕ〜

When Karina grew up, the tsar married her, for he knew he could never find another wife who was nearly as clever."

Max took Rebecca's hand, and she bowed with him as the family clapped. "What an actress!" Max exclaimed. "Our Beckie's a natural talent."

Rebecca could barely breathe. Max thought she was a good actress—and her whole family was clapping for her!

"I'm auditioning for a movie studio this week," Max said. "Maybe I should bring Beckie along!"

Bubbie rolled her eyes. "Don't give her crazy ideas," she said.

Grandpa slapped the table. "Acting is a no-good life for a young lady!"

"Beckie should be a teacher," Papa said, sitting back comfortably. He seemed quite pleased with this idea.

Rebecca's shoulders slumped. Why didn't Papa think she should become an actress? After all, Max said she had talent.

Papa turned to Victor, ending the discussion. "How about working in the store tomorrow?" he asked.

"Tomorrow he comes with me to synagogue," Grandpa declared. He turned to Victor and said sternly, "So close to your bar mitzvah, your Hebrew is not so good!"

Bubbie shook her head at Papa. "Working on Shabbos," she sighed. "Such a shame."

Rebecca knew Jews weren't supposed to work on Saturday, the day of rest. Grandpa worked at the store all week, but on Saturdays he prayed at the synagogue and often took Victor with him.

"I don't like to work on Shabbos, but most people shop on Saturday. I have to keep the store open if I'm going to support the family," Papa said.

Maybe I can't light the candles or go to a movie, Rebecca thought, *but I can help in Papa's store. Then he'll see how grown-up I am.* If she did a good job, maybe Papa would give her a few pennies. That would help her save for candlesticks.

"I'll work tomorrow," she offered.

"I do need help," Papa said. He stroked his mustache thoughtfully. "Why don't we try it?" Rebecca brightened. "Wear your best shoes," he added.

Max sipped his glass of tea. "What do you hear from your brother Jacob in Russia?" he asked Papa. "Now that Russia is fighting against Germany, they are drafting more men. You know the Russian army takes Jewish boys as young as twelve," Max added. "Jacob's family better get out before the war gets worse."

Papa's forehead was creased with lines of worry. "Things in Russia are very difficult," he said with a sigh. He took a letter from his pocket. "This came from Jacob today." He read the letter, changing it into English:

"Dear Brother, I write to tell you that life here is becoming more dangerous as the war spreads. Jews are no longer allowed to work, and I have lost my job. I am afraid to let Josef and Michael out of the house for fear soldiers will snatch them off the street and force them into the tsar's army. Food is scarce, and we are thankful when we have a bit of cabbage soup. Little Ana is sick and weak from hunger, and I fear she will not survive another winter here. A friend will try to smuggle us out of Russia, but it will take every *kopek* we have left. We beg you to send us ship tickets as soon as possible, so we can join you in New York. Our hearts are filled with sorrow, knowing the hardship this expense will cause, but we cannot wait any longer."

Victor's eyes had a faraway look, and Rebecca wondered if he was imagining what his life would be like if he were in the Russian army. She was glad Victor didn't have to worry about that. Grandpa had said that Jewish boys were often treated harshly and given the most dangerous army jobs. Many boys never saw their families again.

"It's no good in the Old Country," Grandpa said. "From now on, we fill the pushke for family."

Max cleared his throat and looked embarrassed. "I wish I could help," he said, "but I can barely pay for the room I'm renting. Somehow, you've got to send them tickets right away."

"I know," Papa said irritably. "We've been trying to save money for a long time."

Sophie looked up. "You don't have to give us our allowance every week," she offered.

Rebecca couldn't imagine what it would be like not to have enough food to eat. She looked at the dishes on the table. They were empty only because her family had eaten as much as they wanted. Rebecca felt ashamed. She couldn't spend money on candlesticks when her cousin was starving.

"I have a little bit saved, Papa," she said. "Maybe that will help buy the tickets."

Papa shook his head. "Don't worry, children. We need much more than your pennies. I'll find a way to raise the money."

⚭⚯⚭

In bed that night, Sadie and Sophie talked until they fell asleep, but Rebecca lay awake thinking about her cousin. Ana must be so frightened. What if she became too sick to escape? The journey from Russia would be long and dangerous. If only Uncle Jacob's family could make it to New York, Rebecca thought, Ana could be like a sister to her. Ana was exactly her age. Why, it would be just like having a twin.

Rebecca could hear Mama and Papa talking softly in
the kitchen. "The ship tickets cost at least thirty dollars
each, and we need to buy five of them. All our savings
won't be enough," Papa said. "And Jacob must have twenty-
five dollars in his pocket to get into America." There was
a long silence. Rebecca added up the numbers in her head.
Papa needed one hundred seventy-five dollars! How would
he ever save that much?

Rebecca crept out of bed and opened her trunk. She
took out the knotted handkerchief that held her savings
and quietly counted. All she had was twenty-seven cents.
Maybe she should give all the money to Papa. But it wasn't
nearly enough to buy even one ship ticket. And Papa had
said he didn't want her savings.

Her wooden dolls lay strewn about in the trunk, where
she had tossed them after dinner. She put them back
together, each doll nestled safely inside the next, but she
held the Beckie doll close as she snuggled under the covers.

"Am I being selfish to want candlesticks for myself?"
Rebecca whispered to her doll. In the dim light from the
kitchen, she could barely see Beckie's painted smile before
she fell asleep.

One for the Money

R ebecca studied the picture on the cover of her sisters' movie magazine. Then she looked again at her own reflection in the mirror that hung in the parlor. She tilted the brim of her hat until it slanted across her forehead. That was just how the movie star Pearl White wore her hat. Rebecca turned her face to one side and then the other, admiring the look. She imagined she was on a movie poster. "Coming Soon! Rebecca Rubin in *The Perils of Pauline!*"

"Stop primping," Mama called. "You'll make Papa late."

"I'm coming!" Rebecca smoothed her cotton stockings and straightened the white collar and cuffs on her dress. Mama always called it her "purple" dress, but Rebecca preferred the elegant description from the mail-order catalog: "Rich violet tweed," it read, "for the sophisticated young lady." Rebecca spit on her finger and rubbed the toes of her matching leather shoes to a shine.

Mama held the leftover hallah from the night before.

As she handed it to Rebecca, she said, "Take this up to Bubbie. Grandpa can have it with his lunch."

"But I'm late," Rebecca complained, running up the stairs two at a time. Through the window on the landing, she glimpsed empty clotheslines strung from the fire escapes. Her Jewish neighbors didn't wash clothes on Saturday. That would be work!

Rebecca opened Bubbie's door and set the bread on the shiny oilcloth that covered the small kitchen table. Sadie and Sophie were in the parlor arguing about how many embroidered napkins they had to make for their wedding chests.

"Napkins, doilies, pillowcases, aprons, tablecloths," Bubbie began, counting on her fingers. "If you don't make them now, you won't have enough linens ready when you start your own home."

"Nobody makes a *trousseau* anymore, Bubbie," Sadie grumbled. "It's 1914 already, and in America you don't need a trunkful of handmade linens to get married!"

Bubbie came into the kitchen holding the calico bag Rebecca used for her crocheting. "You left your needlework here," she said.

Rebecca tucked the bag under her arm. "Maybe if it gets slow in the shoe store, I'll make another doily."

Bubbie frowned. "I don't think you should crochet on

Shabbos—even crocheting is work."

"I'm already helping in the store," Rebecca reasoned.

Bubbie sighed. "I suppose it could be worse," she admitted.

"You'd better take the pattern book," Sadie said. "You'll need the directions."

"I know them by heart," Rebecca said, turning to go.

Bubbie pinched her cheek. "Such a talent with the crochet hook!" She called to the twins, "Your younger sister makes more than both of you for her wedding chest."

"Bully for her," Sadie scoffed.

Rebecca raced down the steps and out the front door. *If I'm old enough to prepare for my wedding,* she thought, *why am I not old enough to go to the movies or light the candles?*

Papa stood on the sidewalk, tapping his foot. Rebecca had wanted the day to be perfect, and already she had spoiled things by being late!

"Sorry, Papa," she began, "I had to fix my hat, and then—"

"My, how dramatic!" Papa smiled, looking at the tilted brim. "So, today you'll be my stylish helper." He put his arm around her shoulder as they walked down East Seventh Street.

"We'll save a little money and skip the trolley," he said. "But we won't save time. It's a long walk."

If Papa didn't want Rebecca's savings, why did he need to save the five-cent fare for the trolley? She tried not to think about the money they needed for cousin Ana and her family. Rebecca had saved so little—how could she make a difference?

Marigolds bloomed in the window boxes on the row houses in Rebecca's neighborhood. As she and Papa walked, the streets became narrower, and storefronts looked out from the ground floor of tenement buildings. They crossed the busy thoroughfare of East Houston Street, and Rebecca admired the elegant window displays in the shops. At last they turned onto Rivington Street. Instead of the usual weekday bustle, just a few pushcarts lined the road. Pungent smells of pickles and cheese and herring filled the air. Neighbors passed each other on the street, and Rebecca heard greetings in many different languages.

When she saw the familiar blue awning of Papa's shoe store, she dashed across the street. Papa caught up to her, out of breath.

"Slow down! You have to watch for wagons, and now there are automobiles, too. Those reckless drivers don't look out for little girls."

Rebecca just grinned and reached for the key in Papa's hand. "Let me do it!" She unlocked the front door and the bell on top jingled cheerily, as if to welcome her. She stepped inside and hung a sign in the window. It said OPEN in English, Yiddish, and Italian. Rebecca hung her hat and shawl in the back room and put her calico bag next to a row of shoe boxes.

"I'll start dusting," she offered, taking the feather duster from its hook. She wanted Papa to see that she could be a big help.

Rebecca breathed in the thick, buttery smell of new leather. She loved the way the shoes sat at attention on the narrow shelves as if they were waiting for the chance to march outside. She whisked the dust from the shoes on display, singing as she worked.

"Take me out to the ball game," she sang. "Take me out with the crowd . . ." In the children's area, she brushed lightly over tiny high-topped boots, thick-soled play shoes, and dainty dress shoes with straps that buttoned across the ankle. "Buy me some peanuts and Cracker Jack, I don't care if I never get back!" She dusted women's shoes with pointy toes, fancy buckles, and squashed heels.

"If the ball game is over," Papa joked, "the sidewalk needs sweeping." He handed Rebecca a tattered broom. "The pushcart peddlers leave such a mess Friday after-noon. I have to sweep up so the store looks better. Put on my workshop apron so your dress won't get dirty."

Rebecca wrinkled her nose. She didn't want to put

the stained canvas apron over her beautiful dress. Then Papa handed her a pair of worn leather boots. "Wear these instead of your good shoes," he told her. Rebecca started to argue, but she didn't want to annoy Papa. She tied on the big apron and replaced her shiny shoes with the old boots.

Outside, Rebecca consoled herself by pretending she was auditioning for the movie studio with Max. She imagined she was playing a poor immigrant who had to sweep the streets to help her family survive. She pushed the broom slowly to show how exhausted she was. She swept up banana peels, soggy potatoes, and pieces of newspaper blowing against the curb. *Life in America is so hard,* she pretended. *I can't go to school but must work every day for pennies!* She hummed a sad Yiddish song.

Lost in her playacting, Rebecca was startled by Leo Berg, a pesky boy from her class at school. His mother walked beside him. Draped around her neck was an elegant fur scarf ending in a fox's head, tail, and paws that dangled from her shoulders. Mrs. Berg swished inside the shoe store without a glance, but Leo stared at Rebecca while she swept.

"This is my father's store," Rebecca said proudly. "I'm helping today."

"Why, you're nothing but a street sweeper," Leo sniffed.

Imagining she was a poor sweeper in a movie was fine,

Rebecca thought, but having someone call her one
was unbearable! Her face burned with anger.

"Sweeping the sidewalk is very important," she
said. "Maybe if you knew how to work hard, you
wouldn't have to wear the dunce cap in school."

Leo's cheeks turned red. "You'd better be
polite, or my mother and I will leave!" He
stepped inside, slamming the door so hard that the glass
pane rattled.

dunce cap

How could she keep quiet when Leo had insulted her?
Yet Rebecca couldn't let Papa lose a customer. She swept
harder and faster, pushing her anger around with the dirt.

When she finished, she walked straight to the back
room and put on her own shoes. As she hung up Papa's
apron, she could hear Leo complaining. Rebecca peeked
through the curtains that screened off the back room.

"These shoes are ugly!" Leo grumbled.

"We've been to every shoe store on Broadway," Mrs.
Berg said. "Leopold didn't like anything!"

Papa sat on a low stool, helping Leo take off a pair of
shoes. Open boxes and shoes were strewn around the
floor. Instead of looking cross, Papa just smiled. "I might
have to show you a special pair I've been saving." He
hesitated. "I don't know if I should. These shoes aren't for
any ordinary boy."

"*I'm* not an ordinary boy," Leo piped up. "What's so special about them?"

Papa rubbed his chin. "Well," he began, "these shoes are made of the same leather used for cowboy boots."

"I want to try them!" Leo demanded. "I see cowboy boots in Western movies every week."

Rebecca fumed. Leo was her age, and he saw movies every week!

"Oh, do show us the cowboy shoes, Mr. Rubin," Leo's mother said. "I'm at my wit's end! If Leopold likes them, I don't care what they cost."

Papa came into the storage room and searched the boxes stacked according to style and size.

"Cowboy boot leather?" Rebecca whispered.

Papa winked. "Boots or shoes, leather is leather," he said.

Rebecca took her bag of crocheting and walked past Leo without glancing in his direction. Sitting near the bright front window, she looped the thick cotton thread around her crochet hook and pulled the stitches through until a lacy flower design took shape.

Mrs. Berg walked around, inspecting the latest women's shoes. "My, my," she clucked. "Aren't you the clever girl! I didn't know anyone still learned to crochet now that so few young ladies make a trousseau." She picked up a satiny shoe with silk bows.

Rebecca wondered if Sadie and Sophie were right. Maybe girls didn't make linens for their wedding chests anymore. She held her doily higher so that Mrs. Berg could admire it. "Well, I'm only nine, and I'm not planning to get married for a long time," Rebecca explained. "But I learned to crochet when I was six, and Bubbie says I have a knack for it."

"That's enough, Rebecca," said Papa. "Let Mrs. Berg browse in peace."

Rebecca pursed her lips. Once again, she had talked too much. If Papa found out what she had said to Leo about the dunce cap, he might send her home!

Mrs. Berg peered closely at the doily. "You couldn't buy such a fine piece for love or money."

Rebecca swelled with pride. Leo's mother was a lot nicer than Leo was. Feeling generous, she took a finished doily from her bag and handed it to Mrs. Berg. "Please take this one," she offered. "I've made so many."

Mrs. Berg patted Rebecca on the head. "What a sweet child." She folded the doily into her purse. "I will certainly enjoy displaying it in our home."

With a dramatic rustle of tissue paper, Papa unwrapped the shoes. He sniffed the leather. "Ah, the aroma of saddles and boots," he said.

Rebecca fought back a giggle. Papa was an actor, too!

Leo grabbed one of the shoes and smelled it.

"All right," Papa said, "try them. But they might not fit." He eased Leo's foot into the shoe with a shiny brass shoehorn.

"They're perfect for me," Leo announced. He put on the second shoe and laced it up himself. Then he tucked his thumbs into the waist of his knickers and strutted around the store with his chest out.

"Doesn't he look handsome in those shoes!" gushed Mrs. Berg. "He'll wear them home."

"Shall I wrap up the old ones?" Papa asked.

"No," Leo said. "Get rid of them."

Papa went to the cash register, and Rebecca began replacing all the shoes in their proper boxes. She hoped Papa would notice how neat everything was.

As Mrs. Berg swept toward the door, she bent down and handed Rebecca something. The bell on the door jingled them out, and Rebecca saw a shiny quarter in her hand. Mrs. Berg had paid her for the doily! She didn't want Papa to see. He might tell her to return the money. Her heart thumped as she hid the quarter in her bag and picked up Leo's old shoes.

"What shall I do with these, Papa? They're hardly scuffed."

"Set them on the workbench," Papa told her.

Rebecca carried a stack of shoe boxes to the back room,

along with Leo's old shoes. As she placed his shoes on the workbench, she saw several other pairs of worn children's shoes lined up near cans of shoe polish. The bench was littered with tools, tiny nails, and scraps of leather.

"What will you do with these old shoes, Papa?" she asked.

Jing-jing! The bell on the door announced a customer before he could answer Rebecca's question. A thin woman with dark braids pinned up around her head stepped inside. A small boy held her hand.

"May I help you?" Papa asked.

"My son's shoes, they are too small," the woman said in a heavy Italian accent. "A friend says to me you have shoes not cost too much?"

"Sit down," Papa smiled. The boy was about the same age as Benny. He had on a pair of worn knickers, and his stockings were mended around the knees. Papa pushed his thumb against the toe of the boy's shoe. "Definitely a bit snug." He took off the old shoes, and Rebecca saw that the soles were worn all the way through. Papa measured the boy's feet with a wooden measuring slide.

"You'd think my little Joey would have plenty shoes," the woman said, "since his father works in shoe factory."

Papa nodded. "I worked in a shoe factory when I first came here from Russia, and I never had a decent pair of my own. I had to put cardboard in my shoes so my socks wouldn't rub the sidewalk!" Papa picked up the boy's old shoes and said, "Let me see what I can do with these."

Rebecca picked up her doily and counted out her stitches, her crochet hook darting in and out. When the boy looked over his shoulder at her, she winked. He giggled and hid his head in his mother's skirt.

Papa returned holding a polished pair of shoes. "I've fixed them up so they hardly look like the same pair." He slipped the boy's feet into the shoes.

"Look, I can wiggle my toes," Joey exclaimed. He skipped around the store.

Rebecca squinted at the shoes as Joey went by. "They certainly *don't* look like the same pair," she remarked, but Papa's stern look silenced her. Why wasn't she supposed to say what was plain as day? She lowered her eyes to her crocheting and moved only her fingers instead of her mouth.

"How much I owe you?" the woman asked.

"Not a penny," Papa said. "I just fixed his shoes up a bit."

"I thank you so much," the woman said with a grateful smile.

Papa patted the boy's shoulder. "Wear them in good

health, Joey." Rebecca watched Joey set off down the street, hopping over cracks in the sidewalk.

"Now you know why I save the old shoes," Papa said quietly. "I keep them for situations just like this."

"Does the lady know what you did?" Rebecca asked.

Papa nodded. "She knows. But it's best not to talk about it, Beckie. No one likes to take charity."

"That was a good thing to do, Papa," said Rebecca. She gave him a hug.

"It's a *mitzvah*," Papa explained. "We should help others whenever we can. Your heart tells you the right thing to do. But you already know that, don't you?"

Rebecca felt a twinge in her own heart as she remembered Ana. Shouldn't she be doing something to help her cousin?

The store grew busier, and thoughts of Ana soon disappeared. As Rebecca carried boxes back and forth, she remembered the quarter in her bag. What if she brought more doilies to the store next week? Maybe Mrs. Berg would come back.

"Papa, could I work with you every Saturday?" she asked.

"We'll see," Papa said. "We'll see."

Two for the Show

On Sunday afternoon, Rebecca stood at the kitchen sink, trying to clean melted wax from the candlesticks. *Why should I have to clean these,* she thought grumpily, *when I can't even light the candles?* She scraped at the wax with her fingernail, wondering how much more money she would need to buy her own candlesticks. With the quarter from Mrs. Berg, she had saved just fifty-two cents. Even if she bargained with the peddlers, that wouldn't be enough. Candlesticks would cost at least two dollars.

She thought again of Ana, and her stomach fluttered. Lighting candles wasn't as important as having enough food to eat. Should she give her savings to Papa for the ship tickets? But Papa had already refused her money and told her not to worry. He would get the tickets soon, wouldn't he?

"'To be, or not to be: that is the question,'" floated a voice from the girls' bedroom. Sadie and Sophie were reading *Hamlet* aloud to each other.

To buy, or not to buy, Rebecca thought. *That is* my *question!*

"*Vroom! Rrroom!*" Benny ran around the parlor holding a toy airplane aloft.

"*Shah!*" Papa hushed him. "Your sisters are studying." He turned the page of his newspaper.

Rebecca walked into the parlor. Through the open window, she could see people strolling along the sidewalks in the mild September air. Neighbors sat on their front stoops, talking and laughing. Victor was off playing stickball, and Mama had gone out. Rebecca didn't want to stay inside tiptoeing around.

She could hear Sadie and Sophie reading Shakespeare's lines with great feeling. But they didn't have an audience, as she'd had when she acted out the folktale with Max. Thinking about performing gave Rebecca an idea. People paid money to see a show! Sometimes children tap-danced right on Orchard Street, between the peddlers' carts, and shoppers tossed pennies to them. Rebecca took Mama's summer straw hat from its hook and put it on. Its wide, floppy brim and big pink flowers would get people's attention.

"I'm going out," she called to Papa from the kitchen. She hoped he wouldn't look up from his paper. Rebecca hurried to the door, but she wasn't quick enough.

"Me, too!" Benny demanded, landing his plane on one of Mama's geraniums.

"Take him with you," Papa ordered, "so the twins can study."

Rebecca's heart sank. Taking Benny would ruin her plan. But her brother happily grabbed his cap and ran down the steps.

The front stoop of their row house was empty. Rebecca saw the sidewalk below her. *Why, the stoop is just like a stage,* she thought.

"I'm going to put on a show," she said to her brother. "So just stay out of the way."

"I want to be in a show, too," Benny said.

Rebecca thought for a moment. If she didn't let Benny help out, he would just keep bothering her. "Tell you what—you can play the organ grinder's monkey," she told him. "You go into the crowd and pass your hat around to collect pennies."

Benny started screeching like a monkey and hopping from one foot to the other. "This is fun!" he cried. "But where's the crowd?"

"We haven't started the show yet," Rebecca explained. "Don't be such a *nudge*, pestering me every minute."

Rebecca stood at the edge of the stoop, right at the top of the steps. She took a deep breath and began singing her favorite song. "Take me out to the ball game, take me out with the crowd . . ."

A few passersby turned to look, but they didn't stop. Rebecca kept singing. Maybe she just had to be patient. Surely a crowd would form soon. She sang louder. But when she finished, no one had stopped, and there were no pennies in Benny's cap.

Rebecca tilted the floppy brim on Mama's straw hat at an angle, like Pearl White's hat. She cleared her throat and began singing at the top of her lungs.

> *I went to the animal fair,*
> *The birds and the beasts were there.*
> *The big baboon by the light of the moon*
> *Was combing his auburn hair.*

Benny hopped up and down, hooting and scratching his chest the way the organ grinder's monkey scratched its fur. A few people paused to watch as Rebecca belted out the end of the song.

> *The monkey he got drunk*
> *And climbed up the elephant's trunk,*
> *The elephant sneezed and fell on his knees,*
> *And what became of the monk,*
> *The monk, the monk, the monk?*

As Rebecca repeated "the monk" over and over, Benny flitted through the thin crowd. Rebecca saw a stout man drop a coin into the hat. Now she was getting somewhere! Maybe a few jokes would bring the people closer. Max had said, "If you make them laugh, your audience will love you."

Rebecca walked down a few steps and began sprinkling the sidewalk with imaginary powder. "Ask me what I'm doing," she whispered to Benny.

"Okay," Benny whispered back. "What are you doing?"

"Louder," Rebecca hissed through her teeth, pretending to look around nervously.

"What are you *doing*?" Benny yelled.

"I'm sprinkling lion powder!" Rebecca announced.

"Lion powder?" asked Benny. "What's that for?"

The crowd drew closer and looked from Rebecca's hand to the steps. More people joined the group.

Rebecca sprinkled with renewed energy. This routine was going well. "Why, it keeps the lions away," she replied loudly.

Benny started laughing, and Rebecca had to prompt him with the next line. But Benny was quick. "I 'member," he insisted. "But there aren't any lions around here!" he shouted to the crowd. The audience chuckled. Benny was a little showman.

Rebecca delivered the punch line. "Well, then, you see how well it works!"

People began to laugh. Benny jumped into the gathering holding out his hat, and Rebecca heard the clink of coins. Suddenly, strong fingers pinched her ear.

"Youch!" she cried. She twisted around and saw Bubbie, who was furiously pulling her up the steps.

"You are shaming us in the neighborhood," Bubbie scolded. "Even Mr. Rossi sees you begging!" Rebecca caught a glimpse of the janitor in the basement apartment scowling at her through his window as Bubbie dragged her along.

"Let go," Rebecca pleaded. "What did I do wrong?"

"You get inside and think about it!" Bubbie said.

"Why is it okay for Max to earn money in a show, but it's not okay for me?"

"Max, Schmax!" Bubbie sputtered. "He doesn't earn two nickels to rub together. Such a man you don't want to be like!"

But Rebecca really *did* want to be a performer, just like Max. She couldn't see anything wrong with earning money by putting on a show.

Rebecca saw her brother pulling out his marbles. His cap was still on the sidewalk. "Benny," she hissed under her breath. "Bring the cap!"

Bubbie led Rebecca into the girls' bedroom and left,

closing the door firmly behind her. Sadie and Sophie looked up from *Hamlet*.

"You're not ready for the stage yet," Sadie laughed, "but the hat is really you!"

Rebecca's cheeks felt hot. "People liked my show," she said. "They even paid for it!" she added as Benny burst into the room and dumped the pennies on her bed. She counted six copper coins. It wasn't much, but it was something. She tied the money into her handkerchief.

"I want some pennies, too!" Benny protested.

"It was my idea," Rebecca argued, "and my show."

"But I did the joke," Benny insisted. "And I got the pennies." Rebecca dropped a penny into his hand. "No fair!" he whined. "You've got more than me!"

"Oh, all right!" Rebecca gave him two more pennies. It was better than having Bubbie come in to settle it. Benny dashed off, and Rebecca looked dismally at what was left. After all that effort, she had just three cents.

Sadie closed her book with a dull thud. "We're going to the park. How can anyone study in this madhouse?"

Rebecca flopped onto her bed. The show had seemed like such a good idea, but Bubbie certainly didn't approve. *Were* the neighbors laughing at her? she wondered. It hardly mattered anyway, since she could never earn much money singing on the stoop. So far, the most she had earned at one time was the quarter she had gotten from Mrs. Berg.

Rebecca buried her pennies in her trunk, pushing aside the neatly folded doilies and linens stored inside. *Imagine saving all these until I'm grown-up,* she thought. She counted all the items she had made—ten pillow covers, seventeen doilies, six long table scarves, and twenty-four napkins. She couldn't use all those linens in her whole life! But seeing the piles of needlework gave her another idea. She packed several items into her calico bag until it bulged.

If Papa would just let her work in the store a few more Saturdays, she'd earn all the money she needed. In just a few weeks, she would stand next to her sisters on Friday night and light candles herself. Everyone would see how grown-up she was. Even Bubbie would be proud of her then.

Solving a Riddle

A month had passed, and Rebecca had worked with Papa every Saturday. Each week Rebecca had improved on her plan to earn money. Now she knew exactly what to do. While Papa bustled between his customers and the back room, she draped a few doilies and pillow covers over a chair. As the ladies strolled by, examining the latest styles, Rebecca hummed and rearranged her pieces.

"How lovely," commented a customer, as she fingered a lacy table runner. "Now that so few girls make a trousseau, it's hard to find handmade items anywhere. My niece just announced her engagement, and this table runner would be a charming gift. Is it for sale?" the lady asked.

"Oh, no," Rebecca said. "I made these myself, and they take so long!"

The lady pulled a quarter from her purse and held it between her gloved thumb and forefinger. "Would this change your mind, dear?" she asked.

"I couldn't," Rebecca murmured. "Papa might be angry."

"It will be our little secret," the lady whispered as she added a dime.

Rebecca quickly folded the table runner into the customer's shopping bag and tucked the coins into her own bag. As Papa stepped out of the back room with a stack of shoe boxes, the lady put her finger to her lips. Rebecca smiled demurely.

This routine had been repeated many times over the past few Saturdays. She wasn't offering to sell her work, Rebecca told herself. If people insisted on buying, it wasn't because she had asked them. She didn't even bargain. She had discovered that people offered more money if you simply said an item wasn't for sale. When she brought her calico bag home each week, it was no longer bulging with doilies and napkins, but it was heavy with coins.

Rebecca replaced several pairs of unwanted shoes in their boxes, smoothed the rumpled tissue paper, and tried to avoid Papa's eyes. He really might be angry if he knew what she was doing. After all, people had come into the store to buy shoes, and she was taking their attention.

"What a fine helper you have," commented an elderly man buying a pair of dressy brogues. "Maybe someday the store will be called 'Rubin and Daughter.'"

Papa smiled proudly. "No, this young lady is going to be a teacher."

Maybe, Rebecca thought. *Or I might be an actress.*

Papa placed the man's box of shoes on the glass case

near the cash register. Inside the case were a few dusty cans of shoe polish and wooden shoe trees to help shoes keep their shape. Rebecca thought doilies would be much prettier to display and sell. But how could she tell Papa without giving away her secret?

"You're awfully quiet this evening," Papa said as they walked home. "I guess being a working girl is more tiring than you realized."

But Rebecca wasn't tired. Her plan to sell her linens had worked better than she had expected. Now she had more than enough money to shop for candlesticks on Orchard Street. At first, her heart had skipped at the happy thought. But then she began to worry about whether she should be selling her trousseau. Her trunk was nearly empty now. Bubbie had been so proud of her needlework—she'd be very upset if she found out Rebecca had sold it.

And something else was bothering her even more. She couldn't stop thinking about Ana, who had to leave Russia soon. How could her cousin make such a long journey when she was weak and ill? Ana would need a lot of courage to face the dangerous escape.

"Papa," she asked, "is cousin Ana still sick? Is she coming to America soon?"

Papa gave Rebecca's hand a squeeze. "Is that what's on

your mind?" he asked. "I'm afraid I haven't heard any more
news about Ana. I've been setting aside as much money as
possible, but we still need a great deal more. I'll send Uncle
Jacob the ship tickets as soon as I can."

Rebecca swallowed, feeling uncertain. The last time she
had offered her savings to Papa, he hadn't wanted her pennies. But now she had a lot more than twenty-seven cents.
In fact, she thought she had enough for real silver candlesticks. If she used her money to buy them, she could finally
light the candles every Friday night. She still wanted to
light the candles as much as ever, but somehow the thought
of buying her own candlesticks had lost its glow.

Rebecca's hand in Papa's felt hot and sweaty. Papa
always said helping others was a mitzvah—something
you should do. She remembered the day in the shoe store
when Papa had said, "Your heart tells you the right thing
to do." Rebecca's heart beat faster in her chest. *Instead of
helping Ana, I've been thinking only of myself,* she realized.
*I've got to give Papa the money I've earned so that he can buy
the ship tickets as soon as possible.*

Rebecca was about to make her offer when a more
troubling thought stopped her from saying a word. Papa
would ask where she got the money. If she told him she
had been selling her needlework in the store, he would be
angry. And what would Bubbie and Mama say when they

found out she had sold her trousseau? Rebecca's throat felt dry. She could never tell them what she had done!

When Rebecca and Papa turned in at their row house, Mr. Rossi was washing chalk from the sidewalk with a long-handled broom. A bucket of brown water stood in a soapy puddle near the stoop. Mr. Rossi cleaned the building in exchange for his rent, but Rebecca thought he acted as if he owned it.

"These kids is always drawing the chalk marks!" he complained. He glowered at Rebecca. "It's you girls making the squares for jumping!"

"*I* wasn't playing hopscotch, Mr. Rossi," Rebecca said. "I was working at my father's store today."

He wiggled his finger in her face. "Today, is not you. Tomorrow, maybe *is* you!"

What a grouch Mr. Rossi was! It wasn't *his* sidewalk, thought Rebecca, and besides, the chalk marks would wash away as soon as it rained. But she couldn't waste time worrying about Mr. Rossi. His problem with the chalk wasn't as important as her problem at all.

All through dinner, thoughts about her empty trunk and Ana and the candlesticks chased each other around in Rebecca's head. Then a horrible thought crept into her mind. Uncle Jacob had said he didn't think Ana could survive another winter. What if her cousin got sicker? What if—what if she died?

I've got to give my money to Papa before it's too late, she thought. But how could she admit what she had done?

Rebecca barely looked up when there was a rhythmic tapping on the door and Max walked in.

"Moyshe," Grandpa said, "you're too late for dinner, but come sit."

Max lifted the lids off the pans on the stove. "First I'll help with the leftover blintzes," he said. "After all, I do want to help out around here."

Mama filled a plate and added a dollop of sour cream. Max sat down and ate hungrily.

"Do you feel like tea?" Bubbie asked him.

"Well, let me see." Max pinched his arm. "No, I don't think I do feel like tea. How about Benny?" He pinched Benny's nose. "Nope, he doesn't feel like tea, either. As for Beckie," he said, pinching her cheek, "you don't feel like tea at all. More like a rosy peach."

A murmur of laughter rippled around the table. Rebecca couldn't even smile. She knew in her heart what she had to do—but why did it have to be so hard? She thought again of Ana and the courage it would take to escape to America. If Rebecca was going to help her cousin, she would have to show some courage, too.

She twisted her napkin in her hand. "Papa," she began in a whispery voice, "I—"

But Max already had Papa's ear. "Believe it or not, I didn't come by just to sponge a dinner from you," he said. "I saw a newsreel at the theater today. The war is spreading fast, and fewer ships are leaving Europe. There's no time to spare if you want to get Jacob and his family out."

"I know, Max," Papa snapped. "I'm doing the best I can."

"You don't understand," Max said, pulling a wallet from his pocket. "I really did come here to help." A wide grin spread across his face. "Remember the audition I had a few weeks ago? Well, you are now looking at Max Shepard, movie actor."

Rebecca stared at Max in amazement. Imagine, a movie actor in her family!

Grandpa lifted his bushy eyebrows. "So, it's a good job?"

"The best!" Max said. "I'll be working steadily and getting paid every week. In fact, I got my first paycheck yesterday." Bubbie gasped as he pulled five crisp ten-dollar bills from his wallet.

"The movie business pays pretty good dough," Max said. "No more borrowing for me! I can pay off my debts and look for my own apartment now." Max handed Papa the money. "I hope this helps buy your brother's tickets."

Papa blinked as if he couldn't believe his eyes. Then he

shook his head and tried to give back the money. "You don't have to do this," he said. "After all, it's not your brother."

But Max wouldn't take it. "Consider it repayment for all the money you've loaned me over the years," Max said. He winked at Mama. "And all the dinners you're going to feed me now that I'm living here in the city."

Papa shook Max's hand and accepted his gift. "This will go a long way," he admitted. "I'll borrow the rest of what we need. It will just take a while to pay it off." Mama leaned over and gave Max a kiss on the cheek.

"And there's one more thing," Max added. "Is it really true that there are people in this family who have yet to see a moving picture?"

"You can put me on that list," Mama said with a smile at Rebecca.

"This is my last weekend working as an usher at the Strand," Max said. "If you come to the matinee tomorrow, I'll get the whole family in free."

Rebecca could barely believe it. There seemed to be no end to Max's surprises.

Bubbie and Grandpa exchanged nervous glances.

"Don't worry," Max reassured them. "It's a Charlie Chaplin comedy. All of you will enjoy it. You'll laugh until your sides hurt!"

Charlie Chaplin

He nudged Rebecca. "And there's an episode of *The Perils of Pauline* with Pearl White."

How Rebecca had dreamed of seeing a moving picture! But tonight Max's surprise didn't make her happy. When Papa and Mama learned what she had done, they would make her stay home, she was sure.

Blinking back tears, Rebecca slipped from the room and returned with her calico bag.

"I have something to tell you, Papa," she said. "Please don't be angry." She took handfuls of change from her bag and dropped them onto the table. Nickels, dimes, quarters, and half-dollars clinked into a pile. Everyone stared at her.

Mama's lips were set in a thin line. "Rebecca Rubin, where did you get this money?"

Rebecca's face burned. She tried not to look at Bubbie. "I—I sold my needlework at the shoe store."

"*Oy vey!*" Bubbie cried. "Your trousseau!"

"I'm sorry," Rebecca said, her eyes downcast.

"How did you do it?" asked Sadie.

"I brought my linens and doilies to the store, and ladies offered me money for them." Tears of shame filled Rebecca's eyes.

Mama shook her head slowly, as if she couldn't believe what Rebecca had done. "Why did you do this?" she asked.

Rebecca answered in a near whisper. "I wanted to buy candlesticks."

"For what you need candlesticks?" Bubbie asked. "One pair isn't enough?"

Rebecca hung her head. "I wanted to light candles on Shabbos, too."

Everyone sat in silence. Rebecca wished she could make herself disappear.

Then Mama came over and lifted Rebecca's chin. "So impatient," she sighed. "I was impatient once, too. I thought I'd never be old enough to welcome the Sabbath. I pretended to light candles using twigs stuck in the ground." She wrapped her arms around Rebecca and held her.

Now that her secret was out, tears of relief and regret rolled down Rebecca's cheeks. "The more things I sold," she sobbed, "and the more money I earned, the less important the candlesticks seemed."

"So," Papa said, "that's what brought on all the secret deals in the shoe store."

Rebecca blinked in astonishment. "You knew I was selling my things?" she asked. "And you aren't angry?"

Papa shrugged. "When your daughter is a successful American businesswoman, what can a father do except sit back and watch?"

Rebecca wiped her eyes and looked at Papa. "What I really want is for Ana and her family to come. I've got more than eight dollars. I know that's not nearly enough for a ticket, but maybe I could sell some more things, and you won't need to borrow so much money."

Suddenly, Sophie spoke up. Her voice was filled with excitement. "Sadie and I have oodles of napkins and doilies and linens. Let's sell some of those, too!" This time it was Sadie who nodded in agreement, her curls bouncing.

Rebecca's face brightened. "You know, Papa," she said, "the display case near the cash register is wasted with shoe polish in it. Let's put the linens there!"

Bubbie sat silently. Now she looked thoughtful. "If people pay to have doilies," she said, "I have a trunkful.

And tablecloths, bed covers, fancy shawls . . . all sitting in a
dark trunk. So, I'll sell a little, too! It's a mitzvah."

Grandpa patted Bubbie's arm. "After all, you're already
married. A trousseau you don't need!"

For the first time in weeks, Rebecca's heart felt light.
Papa didn't mind what she had done. Mama understood
why she had sold her needlework. And Bubbie wasn't
angry. She was even going to help!

"If this works," Papa said, "we'll pay for the tickets in
no time." He put his hand on Rebecca's shoulder. "But you,
young lady, will have to be in charge of handling the mer-
chandise. Do you think you can arrange the display case?"

"I know I can!" Rebecca exclaimed.

Max stood up. In a deep stage voice he said, "In the true
Russian tradition, the youngest daughter has solved the
family's riddle of how to get the money for ship tickets."
He raised his glass of tea. "Here's to Rebecca!"

Bubbie got up and came over to Rebecca. She unhooked
the pin with the leaping hare from her collar and fastened
it to Rebecca's dress. "Keep this, to remember that you are
our own Clever Karina."

Rebecca hugged Bubbie. "Just as long as I don't have to
marry the tsar!" she said.

"Don't worry," Mama laughed. "He'd never have you
without a trousseau!"

Welcome to America

T he days passed slowly as Rebecca waited for cousin Ana's ship to land. She had been worrying about Ana ever since Uncle Jacob's telegram had arrived a few weeks ago. "Escaped Russia with great difficulty. Arriving New York 8 November 1914," the telegram had said. Rebecca knew Ana had been ill. Was her health the "great difficulty" Uncle Jacob had mentioned?

The day of their arrival finally came. Rebecca squinted through the gray fog that blanketed New York Harbor. She could barely see the outline of the brick buildings at Ellis Island. That was where immigrants came when they first arrived in New York. Papa was there now, meeting Uncle Jacob and his family.

Rebecca tugged nervously at her skirt. Had her cousin made it through the difficult voyage? If Ana survived the journey safely, Rebecca was sure they would become as close as sisters. As the wind began to scatter the thin gray wisps of fog, she saw a small ferryboat chugging across the harbor. Behind it, the Statue of Liberty stood out against the clouds.

"Do you think Ana's on that ferry?" she asked, turning to her family. "We've been waiting for hours."

Rebecca's grandparents huddled together against the wind. Bubbie drew her kerchief tighter around her head, and Grandpa pulled his scarf up around his neck. Benny stood on a bench, watching the boats, and Victor held on to Benny's collar so that he wouldn't tumble over.

"It takes a long time to get through Immigration," Mama told Rebecca.

Grandpa shook his head, remembering. "So many people! Such lines! We shuffled into line to get off the ship. We stood in line to go into the building, *schlepping* everything we owned. Then another line while we walked up those steep stairs, praying nobody thought we looked sick."

"I should think *everyone* would feel sick after two weeks sailing across the ocean," said Sadie.

Sophie looked sympathetically at her grandparents. "You must have been so anxious."

Bubbie nodded. "If inspectors thought something was wrong, they might not let us into America."

"When we were on the ship," Mama said, "other passengers warned us about passing through Immigration. Just because you land in New York, it doesn't mean you can live here. The officials keep out anyone who has a serious illness. If they think you have a problem, they mark a letter on your coat with chalk. An *E* means you might have an eye disease. *H* means you might have a heart problem. There's a long list."

Rebecca had heard lots of stories about Ellis Island from her friends at school. When immigrants had a disease that could spread, officials sent them back to the country they came from.

Rebecca remembered what her friend Rose Krensky had told her about immigrants who were sick when they arrived. "*Contagious disease*, they call it," Rose said. "You got one, you go back. That's it. And the ship company has to pay for your ticket." Rebecca tried to forget about Rose's words. She could only hope Ana was well enough to climb the stairs at Ellis Island.

Mama's cousin Max paced along the walkway. "I've got an idea," Max said, flashing his sparkling smile. "Let's practice a little welcoming song to greet the family when they step off the ferry. We'll sing 'You're a Grand Old Flag.'" Max started singing softly.

Rebecca knew the chorus, and so did the twins. Her sisters linked their arms as they chimed in. "You're a grand old flag, you're a high-flying flag, and forever in peace may you wave . . ."

When Rebecca no longer knew the words, she quietly hummed along. She listened carefully as Max sang. He

made every word sound exciting! "You're the emblem
of the land I love, the home of the *free* and the *brave* . . ."
He emphasized some of the words, giving the song more
rhythm. Bubbie nodded in time to the music, and Grandpa
tapped his foot. Benny marched around them in a small
circle, saluting each time he passed Max.

A loud horn blast pierced the
air, and Benny covered his
ears. The ferry pulled up
to the dock, smoke belch-
ing from its smokestack.
Rebecca stretched up on her
toes, trying to see the passengers on deck. Hundreds of
people crowded at the railing in strange-looking clothing—rough black coats, long scarves that fell past their
knees, odd flat caps and summer straw hats. Their arms
were weighed down with feather beds, quilts, and bulging
carpetbags, yet their tired faces glowed with excitement.

"Another boatload of new Americans." Max smiled and
nudged Mama. "Just like we were, not so long ago."

"There's Papa!" Rebecca exclaimed. She jumped up
and down, waving in his direction. Papa had gone to
Ellis Island to sign papers proving that Uncle Jacob and
his family had someone to help them settle in America.
Rebecca searched the crowd anxiously, trying to guess

which girl was her cousin. Even if Ana was sick, the immigration officials wouldn't send her back to Russia alone, would they?

"Start singing," Max directed the family.

Above the din of shuffling feet and shouted greetings in many languages, Rebecca sang with all her might.

"Over here!" Mama called, and Rebecca saw Papa standing next to his brother. Rebecca thought she would have recognized Uncle Jacob anywhere. Although he looked older than Papa, with streaks of gray in his hair and beard, he looked very much like her father. Beside him, Aunt Fanya looked pale and weary. Her shoulders slumped, and her eyes were rimmed with dark circles. A boy a bit taller than Victor waved his hand toward them. He must be either Michael or Josef.

Then Rebecca saw a girl about her own age behind Aunt Fanya. It had to be Ana, but she looked nothing like Rebecca had imagined. Her cheeks were smudged with dirt. Her face looked thin and drawn under her wool scarf, but the rest of her bulged, and her clothes pulled at their buttons. Like the other immigrants, she had a large passenger tag pinned to her coat, which flapped in the breeze.

Rebecca glanced at the crowd behind them. Where was Ana's other brother? Perhaps he was farther back in the crush of people.

Max's voice trailed off, and the musical greeting floated away as the families embraced each other.

"Thank heavens you're here!" Mama said as she hugged Aunt Fanya. Then she looked anxiously at the rest of the family. "Where is—?"

In Yiddish, Aunt Fanya cried, "They've taken Josef!" She began to sob, louder and louder until she was wailing. Strangers paused to look and then quickly turned away. Uncle Jacob put his arm around her shoulders, as if holding her up. Ana clutched her mother's arm and began to cry.

"Josef fell on the ship and hurt his leg badly," Papa explained. "He was limping when he passed through the inspection point, and the officials marked his coat with an L. They separated him from the others and took him away."

It didn't seem possible. Rebecca had worried about Ana making the voyage safely, but she had never imagined that someone else in the family might become sick. Now the officials were holding Josef on Ellis Island and might send him back to Russia! She thought about the mark on Josef's coat.

"Does L mean 'limp'?" she asked Papa.

"It means 'lame.' The doctors are afraid Josef won't be able to walk." A deep frown creased Papa's forehead, but he tried to sound hopeful. He turned to his brother and added in Yiddish, "We'll come back tomorrow and see about getting Josef released. If all goes well, the Ellis Island doctors can treat him, and he'll be better soon."

Aunt Fanya tugged weakly at Papa's arm. "Don't let them send him back!" Her eyes were filled with fear.

"Don't worry," Papa said gently. "I'll go to the Hebrew Immigrant Aid Society. They'll know what to do."

Rebecca offered Ana her handkerchief. "Don't cry," she said in Yiddish. "Papa will help." But she knew from what Rose had told her that getting Josef through Immigration wouldn't be easy.

Mama took the ship tags off the family's clothing, and they all set off down the street, clutching bundles to their chests. Cousin Max held Benny's hand and carried a big brass *samovar* under one strong arm. Rebecca's family had a samovar from Russia, too. Samovars were used for making tea. Grandpa had always told Rebecca that a samovar was a family's treasure and something they tried not to leave behind.

Papa and Uncle Jacob carried a large trunk between them. As they walked, Papa explained how horseless trolleys worked. Mama told Aunt Fanya about cooking on a gas stove. Victor tried to explain the game of baseball to Michael, batting at the air to demonstrate.

As always, the twins walked together,

samovar

talking and giggling, but for once, Rebecca didn't mind. She usually hated it when her sisters left her out, but now she had Ana by her side. She balanced a heavy bundle against her chest and hooked her arm through Ana's, pointing out a huge theater with glittering lights.

"We have movies here," she said. "You watch the actors moving on a screen instead of on a stage." Ana's large brown eyes grew wider. Rebecca had so much to share with her cousin and could barely contain her happiness now that she had arrived. Although she was concerned about Josef, she was relieved that Ana's health was better. With fresh food from the markets, Ana would grow stronger every day. From now on, they would be together all the time.

When they entered their building, a cat dashed from the entrance down into the basement. "That's Pasta," Rebecca told Ana. "She belongs to Mr. Rossi, who takes care of the building. He says Pasta is the only cat who likes spaghetti more than chasing mice!"

Ana frowned. "Not know these words," she said. Before Rebecca could explain, Mama spoke.

"I know you all want baths," said Mama with a smile as they crowded into the apartment. "Louis," she said to Papa, "take your brother and Michael to the bath house." She handed Papa two towels, a small cake of soap, and a neatly tied bundle of fresh clothes. Then she pulled the metal washtub from under the sink and set it in the middle of the kitchen. She started filling a bucket with hot water.

"Hot water pours from the faucet?" Aunt Fanya marveled. "Right in the kitchen?"

Mama nodded. "The ladies will have their baths here. Everyone else, scoot!"

Bubbie herded the rest of the family upstairs. "I'll make tea," she said, "and I've got a big plate of rugelach." Max licked his lips.

Rebecca could wait until later for Bubbie's flaky cinnamon pastry. She wasn't going to leave Ana now. "I'll help with the baths," she announced.

Ana untied her scarf, and Rebecca was delighted to see that her cousin's hair was the same rich brown shade as her own. They already looked almost like twins!

Layers of blouses, skirts, and sweaters lay beneath Ana's bulging buttons. By the time she had shed everything except her slip, Ana looked like a scrawny chicken that had lost all its feathers.

"We not have room to pack many things," Ana said in halting English. "I wear all clothes."

"How did you learn to speak English?" Rebecca asked. "You speak very well."

"In Russia, we have boarder who teach us English," Ana said proudly. "I learn fastly."

Mama looked doubtfully at the pile of dirty clothes. Rebecca knew that puffy peasant blouses and long skirts with bands of embroidery along the hem would mark Ana as a *greenhorn*. That was the insulting term some Americans called newcomers just off the boat.

"Instead of washing these," Mama said, "I think you'll want to replace them with American clothes."

Aunt Fanya looked horrified. "Throw away clothes?"

Mama nodded. "I'm sure the ship was riddled with lice."

Rebecca shuddered at the thought of bugs crawling in her clothes. "I've got the perfect dress for Ana," she exclaimed. "In fact, with hand-me-downs from the twins, I've got two of everything! Ana and I can dress exactly alike."

"Now you're *Amerikanka*," Mama said to Fanya. "An American. The first thing to do is dress like one." She splashed a final bucket of hot water into the tub.

Ana stepped in and began scrubbing away weeks of grime and sour ship smells. "On ship, we must wash with salty seawater," she said. "Now water in tub is Ana soup!"

Rebecca laughed at the joke. Ana really did speak English pretty well. Rebecca sat down next to her aunt. "Now you should have an American name," she said. "May I call you Aunt Fannie?"

"Fannie," repeated her aunt. In Yiddish, she said, "I like

this American name. I will dress American, and learn to speak it, too—if I stay." She twisted the fringe on her scarf and looked down sadly. "If Josef is sent back, we all go back together."

Ana stopped scrubbing, and her eyes brimmed with tears. "We can't go back to Russia," she said hoarsely. "It's too far. Papa can't work there, and Michael and Josef have to hide in the house from the tsar's soldiers."

Aunt Fannie began to cry, her shoulders shaking.

Mama put her arms around her. "Even if there were enough money for new tickets," she said gently, "there's no life for you in Russia anymore." She looked steadily at Aunt Fannie. "I'm afraid there's no going back."

A cold feeling grew in Rebecca's stomach. The pile of clothes seemed like the Russian life Ana and her family had to throw away. But if Russia wasn't safe, how would Josef survive if he was sent back alone?

A Yiddish Mistake

R ebecca felt warm and cozy in her bed, and when she opened her eyes, she remembered why. There was Ana, sound asleep beside her, with Rebecca's wooden doll, Beckie, smiling between them. *Now I've got a twin, just like my sisters,* she thought happily. She patted Ana's shoulder.

"Wake up," she said. "We're going to school!" Ana stretched sleepily, kicking Rebecca's ankles, but Rebecca didn't mind. "We can dress exactly alike," she announced. She pulled matching skirts and sweaters from the closet and laid out stockings, shoes, and hair ribbons. "Don't be nervous about school," Rebecca said. "We're going to stay together the whole time." She brushed out her cousin's hair and tied on a fluffy bow. Then Ana did the same for her before they went into the kitchen.

"You two must think you're looking into a mirror," Mama exclaimed. "You look so alike, it's like having two sets of twins in the house!" Rebecca beamed, and Ana gave a shy smile.

Sadie urged Benny up from the chairs he slept on each

night. Papa always pulled two chairs together for him and covered them with soft blankets. Now, every chair was needed at the table. The apartment was crowded with the new family. Victor usually slept on the couch in the parlor, but he had let Michael take that spot. Instead, Victor had spent the night on a feather bed that Mama spread on the floor. Uncle Jacob and Aunt Fannie had slept upstairs in Bubbie and Grandpa's parlor, but they came down to help Michael and Ana get ready for school.

Mama set glasses of coffee mixed with milk on the table beside a heaping plate of sweet rolls. "When Josef comes, we'll put another feather bed on the floor," she said.

If *he comes,* Rebecca thought.

Aunt Fannie looked at the coffee and rolls. "No tea?" she asked. "And what about soup?"

Rebecca giggled. "We don't have soup for breakfast in America! And we drink coffee in the morning." She stirred a lump of sugar into a glass of warm coffee milk and handed it to Ana.

After one sip, Ana smiled. "Is tasty!" she assured her mother. "America is land of milk and honey!"

As soon as one person finished eating, Mama washed the dishes and quickly refilled them for someone else. Rebecca could barely move around the crowded kitchen, and there was no place for her to sit. As she stood near the warm stove eating her roll, there was a knock at the door. Papa opened it to find Mr. Rossi scowling at him.

"*Scusi*, Mr. Rubin," the janitor said, "but you know is against the rules to take in boarders here."

Papa appeared calm as he answered, but Rebecca saw his mustache twitch in anger. "Don't worry, Mr. Rossi, these aren't boarders. This is my brother and his family. They just got to America yesterday. They'll be getting settled on their own very soon." Papa smiled slightly. "You know how hard it is when you first arrive in New York!"

Mr. Rossi only grumbled. "A few days, okay, but no more. Otherwise, I have to report to the landlord. I come check again. I'm sorry, but it's my job." He left, and Papa closed the door.

"Where will we go?" Aunt Fannie asked, speaking in Yiddish.

"I'm going to start looking for a job today," Uncle Jacob said. "We don't want to cause trouble for you, Louis. I'm a good cabinetmaker, and I hope to find work and a place to live as quickly as possible."

"You'll stay here as long as necessary," Papa reassured him. "If we have trouble with Mr. Rossi, I'll speak to the landlord myself."

"What a grouch," Rebecca said under her breath. Mr. Rossi always seemed to be griping about something.

He even complained that Pasta didn't catch enough mice.

Still, she couldn't help feeling a bit worried. Now he was causing trouble for Ana and her family. Rebecca had waited so long for Ana to arrive, and if Mr. Rossi made them move, she would lose her new twin. Mr. Rossi couldn't make them leave, could he?

Mama gave each of the children a lunch box and handed Aunt Fannie her scarf. "I'll help you register Michael and Ana at school," she said. "Be sure to bring their immigration papers along."

Uncle Jacob patted his son on the head and beamed. "The best thing in America is free schools that everyone can attend," he said. "I hope Michael can keep going to school and not have to work."

"He's too young to have a job," Papa explained. "In New York, children must stay in school until they are fourteen years old."

Uncle Jacob sighed. "Thirteen or fourteen," he said, "makes no difference. If Josef can't help us earn a living, then Michael will have to work."

"Well, let's hope for the best," Papa said. He turned to Mama. "When you take Fanya to register the children, don't let the school put them with the first-graders just because their English isn't perfect. They'll catch on quickly."

"Please make sure Ana stays in Miss Maloney's

classroom with me," Rebecca pleaded. "Ana and I are going to be like a new pair of shoes—always together!"

Outside, Mama and Aunt Fannie led the way, while Victor, Michael, and the girls followed in the brisk morning air. "Look, there's my friend Rose!" Rebecca said. "She moved here from Russia last year." They hurried to catch up, and Rebecca introduced her cousin.

Rose's hair was in tight braids, with a blue ribbon tied at the end of each one. "Have you ever been to school?" Rose asked Ana.

Ana shook her head. "At home my papa teaches me to read and figure numbers. But I'm speak English."

Rose wagged her finger in the air. "I'll give you a piece of advice. Don't speak a single word of Yiddish in school."

"Piece of advice?" Ana repeated. "Piece of paper, I know. Piece of bread, this I know. What is 'piece of advice'?"

"Oh, brother," Rose laughed. "You're going to have your hands full, Rebecca."

As the girls arrived at school, Ana hung back. "Is so big," she whispered, gazing up at the huge brick and stone building that nearly spanned a city block.

"Welcome to P.S. 64," Rebecca said. "The *P* stands for 'public,' which means everyone who lives here can attend for free. And the *S* just stands for 'school.'"

"In New York," Rose explained, "the neighborhood schools have numbers instead of names. We're lucky to go to P.S. 64, because it's nearly new."

Rebecca took Ana's hand and led her to the girls' entrance. "This is where we go in," she explained. "The boys have a different door. In the classroom there's a closet to hang up our things. You and I can share a hook."

Miss Maloney stood at the door, her hair in a puffy pompadour and her shirtwaist and skirt crisply pressed. Mama and Aunt Fannie waited politely to one side while the girls lined up.

"Silence, please," the teacher reminded the chattering girls. "Proceed into the school like young ladies."

Rebecca put her finger to her lips, and her cousin understood right away. Ana was smart, Rebecca thought, and would quickly catch on to the school routine.

As the girls filed in, Miss Maloney put her hand on Ana's shoulder. "And who are you?"

"That's my cousin," Rebecca explained. "She just came from Russia yesterday. She's exactly my age, Miss Maloney. I can help her if she stays with me."

The teacher looked uncertainly at Ana. "Your parents must register you at the office," she said. "You might belong in the class for immigrants who need to learn English."

Mama stepped forward and introduced herself and Aunt Fannie. "I'll help Mrs. Rubin with all the paperwork," she said, "and we expect Ana will do fine in a regular class, as long as Rebecca is nearby to help her out."

"I'm speak English," Ana declared. She cleared her throat. "My name is Ana Rubin. I have nine years. I can write English alphabet."

Miss Maloney crossed her arms and tapped her finger thoughtfully. Then she turned to Mama. "We'll try it for a few days, but if it doesn't work out, she'll have to go into a lower grade, or the special class." She looked at Rebecca. "Help your cousin learn the routine, but I want no unnecessary talking, and you must speak only in English. Otherwise Ana will never learn."

"I'll take care of her," Rebecca promised as Mama and Aunt Fannie set off for the school office. Rebecca was filled with excitement as she showed her cousin where to store her lunch box. Ana was going to be in school with her every day!

Miss Maloney moved one of the students so that the girls could sit side by side at the wooden desks bolted to the floor. She made a quick check to see that the students' hands and faces were clean and their hair neatly combed. The pupils showed her their clean white handkerchiefs. Then Miss Maloney stood at the front of the room.

"Class," she began, and the students sat up straight with their hands folded on their desks. "Since it's Monday morning, and your minds have probably been quite idle during the weekend, we shall begin with some arithmetic teasers. Leo Berg, you are class monitor this week."

Leo walked around importantly and handed out blank paper at the beginning of each row of desks. When he reached Ana's row, he smirked at her. "Greenie," he said under his breath.

Ana didn't understand what Leo had said and didn't know it was an insult. She gave him a friendly smile. Rebecca fumed. Leo was so nasty!

Ana leaned over and whispered, "What is 'teaser'?"

Rebecca tried to explain quietly. "Miss Maloney gives us numbers to add and subtract. She does it out loud, very fast. We have to do the problem in our heads and then write down the answer." Ana looked puzzled.

Miss Maloney began the exercise, speaking rapidly. "Three plus five, minus two, plus six." The students all wrote down their answers, except for Ana. She tapped Rebecca's arm as Miss Maloney launched into the next problem. Rebecca tried to ignore her cousin and concentrate, but by the time Miss Maloney had gotten halfway through the new problem, Rebecca was impossibly lost. She had to leave the answer blank.

"Just add and subtract each number in your head," she explained again. But Ana still didn't understand. Maybe she didn't know the meaning of the words "add" and "subtract," Rebecca thought. There was only one way to make it clear. Covering her mouth and whispering softly, Rebecca began to explain the exercise in Yiddish. She hadn't spoken more than three words when Miss Maloney slapped her ruler against the desk. Rebecca was so startled that she nearly jumped out of her shoes.

"Rebecca Rubin," Miss Maloney said. "Come up here immediately."

Rebecca approached the teacher's large oak desk. "I only needed to give her the directions—"

But Miss Maloney wouldn't listen. "You know the rules," she said. "There is no place in this school for any language except English." She took the dunce cap from a shelf and plopped it on Rebecca's head.

Rebecca walked slowly to the tall stool in the corner of the room, in front of everyone. Her face burned with shame. Leo snickered, and his friends joined in. Soon the entire class was laughing at her. When Rebecca dared to look up, she saw Ana giggling and pointing at the dunce cap.

Her heart sank. Even her cousin was making fun of her! It was the worst punishment Rebecca could imagine. Only Rose looked on with sympathy.

At lunch, Rebecca could barely eat. How could her cousin have laughed at her? When Ana complained about the food Mama had given them, Rebecca ran out of patience.

Ana frowned at her bagel. "In Russia we eat bagels when somebody die."

"Bagels aren't just for funerals," Rebecca said curtly. Maybe Ana was afraid it would be bad luck to eat a bagel while Josef was sick at Ellis Island, but Rebecca was too angry to care. "Don't be superstitious," she snapped.

Ana looked confused. She clearly did not understand what Rebecca meant about being superstitious, but she chewed her bagel without another word.

"Greenie! Greenie!" taunted Leo and his friends as they passed by. "Yiddish-talking greenie!"

Rebecca jumped up and yelled back, "Meanie! Meanie! Big fat wienie!" Wienie was short for wienerwurst, a German sausage. That was a good name for Leo, thought Rebecca with satisfaction.

Rose pulled her down. "Ignore them," she said. "You'll only get into more trouble. How many mistakes do you want to make today?"

Rebecca turned her back on the boys. "Even Ana laughed at me," she muttered to Rose, still smarting from the shame. "And I spoke Yiddish to help her!"

"Ana saw the others laughing and thought it must be

a joke," Rose explained. "She doesn't know what a dunce cap is."

"What Ana not know?" Rebecca's cousin asked.

"The pointy hat Miss Maloney put on Rebecca is called a dunce cap," Rose told her. "Dunce means 'stupid.' It's a punishment for breaking the rules. Rebecca broke the rules by speaking Yiddish in school."

Ana turned pale. "I *not* know!" she protested. "I am sorry, Rebecca. Don't be mad on me."

Rebecca forced a little smile. She didn't want to be angry with her cousin. She wanted to be as close as twins, but now she realized that it wasn't always going to be easy. Even Sadie and Sophie argued sometimes.

"School is difficult," Ana sighed. "My English not good."

"Don't worry," Rose told her as they finished eating. "I didn't even know American letters when I first came. Now English is as easy for me as Yiddish. And you're lucky Miss Maloney didn't change your name." She closed her lunch box, and they headed back to their classroom.

"Get different name at school?" Ana asked.

"Oh, sure," Rose said. "Teachers do it all the time. In Russia, my name was Rifka." Ana nodded as if she knew that name. "But on the first day of school, they call me Rose. I was afraid to tell my parents. Then one day the teacher sends home a note. My mother reads it and says,

'Who is this Rose?' When I tell her it's me, she gets so mad!" Rose shrugged. "At home, I'm still Rifka, but here, I am Rose."

Ana shook her head. "I not like to have two names," she said.

As the girls settled at their desks, Rebecca thought about Aunt Fannie. Was it wrong to give someone an American name? Her aunt had seemed pleased when Rebecca suggested the name Fannie. Her grandfather wanted to be called "Grandpa" instead of the Yiddish word, *Zayda*. And Max had changed his own name from Moyshe. Maybe it was only wrong when it wasn't your choice. How hard it must be to move to another country!

Miss Maloney smoothed her white shirtwaist and clasped her hands primly. "Boys and girls, our class has been chosen to present the morning assembly on Friday. The school has received a new American flag, and we will recite some poems to honor the occasion. Who can tell me how many stars are on the new flag, and why?"

Sarah Goldstein's hand shot into the air. She stood up when Miss Maloney called on her. "In 1912, Arizona and New Mexico became states. Now there are forty-eight stars on the flag," she said.

"That is correct, Sarah," said the teacher. She pointed to the poetry book she kept on her desk. "Tomorrow I will assign each of you a poem about the flag. You must memorize it by Thursday."

Lucy Valenti raised her hand and asked, "Can we sing a song, too?"

"There's no time for the class to learn a song," Miss Maloney said.

The class groaned with disappointment. "Oh, *please*, Miss Maloney," several students begged.

Miss Maloney thought for a moment. "It might be a good ending to the program. If one of you knows a suitable patriotic song, I'll consider it," she said. "We'll audition tomorrow, and I'll choose one singer only."

How wonderful it would be to sing on the stage, in front of the entire school! All afternoon Rebecca wondered which song she could prepare by tomorrow. Maybe she could learn the song Max had sung when Ana arrived. It was about a flag, and she already knew some of it.

When school ended for the day, several excited girls crowded together.

"I'm going to sing 'The Star-Spangled Banner,'" Sarah said. "It's all about the flag."

"I'll sing 'Yankee Doodle Dandy,'" Lucy chimed in. "It's not about the flag, but it's very patriotic."

"What means 'patriotic'?" Ana asked.

"That's easy," said Sarah. "It means you love your

country and would do anything to defend it."

Ana looked confused. "I love land of Russia," she said, "but I never love tsar, and my brothers won't go in Russian army to fight."

"But now you love America," said Rebecca.

"Maybe someday," Ana said, "if America lets my brother Josef stay. How can immigration men send him back to Russia just because leg is hurt? Is not right."

Rebecca had to agree. It *wasn't* fair to hold Josef. If he had injured his leg *after* he had landed in New York, no one would think of sending him back to Russia. But Ana was here to stay, and Rebecca hoped she would love her new country. Maybe being part of the assembly would make her feel more American. Rebecca would try to help.

Music for a Song

CHAPTER 8

The girls all left school together, but Rebecca kept walking after her friends turned the corner for home. "I've got some shopping to do," she announced to Ana.

"You have money for buying?" Ana asked.

Rebecca jingled four pennies in the pocket of her sweater. She had told Mama she might treat Ana to a seltzer, but she could do that another day. As long as Mr. Rossi didn't cause trouble, Ana would be living with her for a long time, and today Rebecca needed something important.

"I've got to find the words and music to the song I want to sing at school," she said. "Just wait till you see all the pushcarts on Orchard Street. You can buy anything there. Each peddler sells something different. Pickles, fish, apples, pots and pans, cloth, hats—and music!"

The sun had warmed the afternoon air, and the girls strolled arm in arm. "That's Mr. Goldberg's candy shop," Rebecca said, pointing to a store with a striped awning over the front window and displays of candy-covered almonds and fancy chocolates. "He makes the best egg creams and plays the best music."

"What is egg cream?" Ana asked.

Rebecca squeezed her cousin's arm. "Oh, Ana, you're in for a treat. I'll take you when I get my allowance next Saturday. An egg cream is a chocolate-flavored soda. There's no egg in it, or cream," she explained, "but there's milk, and it has a big, bubbly top. It's smooth!"

"Smooth?" Ana repeated.

Rebecca smiled, thinking of how often her older sisters used the word. "*Smooth* means 'modern and wonderful,' all at once!"

"American way of speaking is strange," Ana observed. "Smooth means wonderful, and egg cream has no egg and no cream!" The girls giggled.

They walked until they came close to the towering tenement buildings that crowded the Lower East Side. Ana stood still. "Is dark here," she said. "Not smooth."

Horse-drawn wagons crowded the streets, and horse droppings littered the road, their foul smell rising in the air. Boys in large-brimmed hats pitched bottle tops against a tall stoop. They punched and jostled each other, laughing loudly. As the girls walked farther, the crowds grew thicker, and soon it seemed to Rebecca as if she and Ana were pushing against every person who had ever come to

America. Ana gripped Rebecca's arm when a train clattered by on elevated tracks with a deafening roar.

"People live here?" Ana asked, peering into the dark, open hallway of a tenement building. Smells of boiled cabbage filled the air.

"Bubbie, Grandpa, and Mama lived near here when they first came to America," Rebecca said. "The rent is cheap." She pointed high up at a sooty window behind a fire escape. "Mama and Papa lived right there when they first got married, and even after Sadie, Sophie, and Victor were born." Rebecca was glad they now lived blocks away in their row house, with large windows facing the front and the back. Even on the hottest days, fresh air moved through the apartment. "Don't worry," Rebecca reassured her cousin. "You're not going to live here—just shop."

As they turned onto Orchard Street, the din of many voices rose about them almost as loud as the roar of the train. Pushcart peddlers shouted out what they had to sell, and shoppers touched, squeezed, argued, bargained, and bought.

"I hear Yiddish!" said Ana, as her face lit up with pleasure.

"Sure," Rebecca laughed. "Practically everyone here speaks Yiddish."

So many pushcarts lined the street

that there was room for no other traffic than the people who trudged along on foot. Women carried large baskets or oilcloth bags bulging with potatoes, cabbages, and carrots. Knots of men stood and talked, gesturing with their hands.

"What are yellow things?" Ana asked, pointing to a cart piled high.

"Why, those are bananas," Rebecca said. "Haven't you ever eaten one?" Ana shook her head, but Rebecca didn't stop to explain. "There!" she exclaimed, pointing just ahead. "That man is selling sheet music." Rebecca stepped up to the cart, peering inside. "I'm looking for 'You're a Grand Old Flag,'" she told the peddler.

"Oy, such a little thing and already buying music," said the peddler, sifting quickly through the piles of colorful sheet music. "I'll bet you're playing the piano. In the tenements, they got practically nothing to eat, but a piano they got!"

Rebecca shook her head. "My teacher will play the piano. I'm going to sing in a school assembly." At least she hoped she was. Right now, she needed the words to the song to even have a chance.

The peddler pulled a red, white, and blue cover from deep under the jumbled pile. "The great music of George M. Cohan!" he bellowed. "*Mazel tov!* Congratulations!

Today is your lucky day. A special price I'm giving on sheet music. So today you'll take this almost new copy for only ten cents."

"Ten cents?" Rebecca gulped. But she knew you never paid the asking price for anything on Orchard Street. She thought about how Bubbie got the peddlers to lower their prices. Bubbie argued and sometimes even insulted them, although nobody seemed to take it seriously.

"A robber!" Rebecca yelled. "A robber trying to trick a little girl!"

"Shah!" scolded the peddler. "You want to scare away all my customers?" He waved the sheet music just out of her reach. "Look at how perfect. Every page is here, and there isn't so much as a crease on the cover. So, I'll make you a bargain like you never heard. Take it home for just seven cents!"

"You think I'm a millionaire?" Rebecca asked, stalling for time. How could she get the man to lower the price again?

Ana's eyes were wide. "How much money do you have?" she whispered.

"Not that much!" Rebecca whispered back.

But the peddler heard every word, as if his hearing was tuned to the sound of each pigeon feather that dropped onto the sidewalk. "For such a talented singer, I'll give it away practically free for a nickel!"

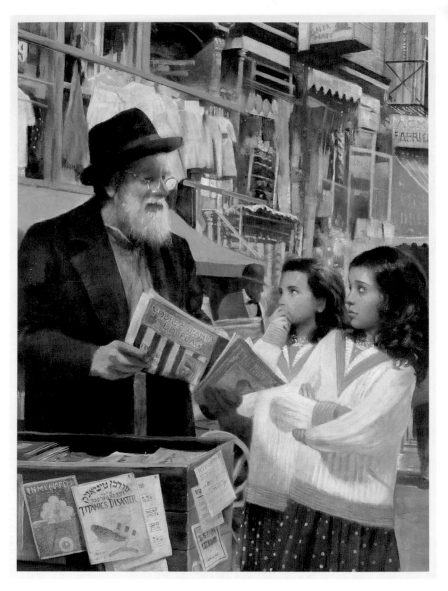

"There's a tear on the back cover," Rebecca said. "Two cents."

Rebecca looked at the music. Here were the words she needed and the notes Miss Maloney could play on the piano in the assembly hall, if only she chose Rebecca to sing! She fingered the pennies in her pocket.

"There's a tear on the back cover," she said, folding her arms. "Two cents."

"You want my children should starve in the street?" yelled the peddler. He put his hand over his heart, as if it were breaking.

If the peddler was going to be dramatic, Rebecca decided that might work for her, too. She pulled out her handkerchief and sniffled into it. "I can only spend three pennies," she whimpered, handing the music back. "Here, mister. I don't have to sing at the assembly." She looked up with sad eyes and started to leave. Ana patted her shoulder sympathetically, but as they walked away, Rebecca winked at her.

"Such children!" the peddler cried. "Like my own little girls. So you'll take it for three cents! This week I won't eat."

Rebecca beamed. She quickly handed over the pennies and took the sheet music. Then she steered Ana back to the banana peddler.

"I have here a young lady who has never eaten a banana," she said. "How many for one penny?" The man handed Rebecca two ripe bananas.

Ana spoke up. "That's all?" she asked, sounding

insulted. "Only two for a whole penny?"

Rebecca stared in amazement. Her cousin really did catch on quickly.

The man handed Rebecca two green bananas. "Two for now, two for tomorrow," he said.

Rebecca paid her penny. She handed a ripe banana to her cousin, who promptly bit into the skin.

"No, no!" Rebecca cried. "Don't eat that." She peeled her banana to expose the fruit, and Ana did the same. "Now try it," Rebecca said.

Ana took a big bite. "Is wonderful," she said. "Fruit with its own wrapping! And I get four bananas for price of two."

Rebecca grinned. "That's what I call bargaining! Don't ever pay what they ask," she advised. "It's the first rule of living in New York."

"We play game with peddlers," Ana laughed. "We are smooth!"

Two Songbirds

Rebecca barely slept at all Monday night, going over the words to the song in her head. She didn't want to forget them in the middle of the audition! Tuesday morning she dressed quickly, eager to get to school. She tucked her doll into her pocket. "Wish me luck," she whispered to the wooden Beckie doll.

The morning routine was as hectic as it had been the day before. First Rebecca had to wait her turn to use the toilet in the hallway, then wait for a chance to wash at the sink, and finally wait for a chair to sit down for breakfast.

Papa and Uncle Jacob talked rapidly in Yiddish. "I went to all the builders, and none of them wanted a cabinetmaker. No one wants to hire a new immigrant," Uncle Jacob said. "One man told me to try the garment factories." He shrugged. "I suppose if I can cut a board, I can cut a piece of cloth."

"You don't want to work in a sweatshop," said Papa. "It's not healthy, and the pay is terrible." His forehead creased into a frown. "I wish the shoe store had more business. Then you could work with me."

"I know," Uncle Jacob said. "But you've done enough, Louis. I'm willing to take any job for a start."

As the girls headed off to school, Rebecca stopped in the entry to tuck the sheet music safely inside her coat. Outside, a cold drizzle fell, and the girls stepped up their pace.

"Today my papa is looking again for job," Ana said. "And your papa is going to Hebrew Immigrant Aid Society." Ana's face was pale. "I am afraid for my brother if infection on leg doesn't go away."

Rebecca couldn't think of anything to say. Ana was right—it made no sense that an injured leg could keep a boy out of the country. Besides, if Josef was too sick to stay in America, how could he go back to Russia alone?

She tried to take her mind off Josef by thinking about the audition. If just one of her classmates sang better than she did, Rebecca wouldn't be chosen to sing in the assembly.

As soon as the class had recited the Pledge of Allegiance, the students sat with their hands folded on their desks.

"We're going to start right off with the audition," Miss Maloney said. "We have very little time to prepare for this assembly, and I want it to go perfectly." She looked around the room. "Who would like to try a song?"

Five students raised their hands, including Rebecca.

Two boys started off, and each one sang in a high, clear voice. But their songs had nothing to do with the flag or America. Rebecca was next.

Leo hid behind a book and stuck out his tongue at her. Rebecca turned her eyes away. She wasn't going to let Leo ruin her audition. She reached into her pocket and patted Beckie for luck. Then she sang out with a big smile. She imitated Max, giving the song rhythm. The other students began to clap along with her singing. When she got to the last words of the song—"Keep your eye on the grand old flag!"—she gave a sharp salute.

But Miss Maloney only said, "Thank you, Rebecca." Next, Sarah sailed through "The Star-Spangled Banner," but her ending was off-key. Finally, Lucy sang "Yankee Doodle Dandy." Rebecca's heart beat faster as Miss Maloney made her decision.

"I think you've all voted with your clapping," she said at last. "While each of our singers did well, I like the enthusiasm you showed for Rebecca's lively song. It seems just right for the assembly. It will be our grand finale!" Miss Maloney picked up a stack of papers. "Now I'll pass out some poems for you to learn. Since there are forty-two students in our class, each poem will be recited by two students together."

Rebecca squeezed her doll through her pocket and thought, *I'm going to sing for the entire school!* She pictured herself standing on the stage, singing along with the gay notes of the piano. She could almost hear the applause.

"Pay attention, Rebecca!" Miss Maloney was standing in front of her. Rebecca blinked as Miss Maloney repeated her words. "These poems are too hard for Ana, and I can't take a chance on anyone making mistakes at the assembly. Instead, I've decided to have her sing with you. I'm trusting you to teach her the song at home."

Rebecca was speechless. She had worked so hard for the chance to sing a solo, and now she would have to share it with her cousin. Immediately, she felt ashamed of her selfish thoughts.

Beside her, Ana opened the sheet music. "You're grend old fleg," she murmured.

Why, Ana can barely pronounce the words! thought Rebecca with alarm. Miss Maloney had said she couldn't take a chance on anyone making a mistake. What if Ana did? It would be so embarrassing!

Miss Maloney turned to write on the blackboard, and Lucy passed Rebecca a crumpled note. As Rebecca unfolded it, she glanced up. Lucy looked as if she was about to cry.

"No fair!" the note said. "Ana doesn't even know the song. She shouldn't get to sing."

Lucy must feel terrible, thought Rebecca. Lucy had auditioned, yet she wouldn't get to sing at all. Rebecca felt sorry for her friend, and she hoped Lucy wasn't blaming her. She stuffed the note into her pocket before Miss Maloney caught her.

Rebecca couldn't keep her mind on her work, and she was grateful when Miss Maloney took the class up on the roof for some exercise. The rain had stopped, and pale sunlight pushed through the clouds. Rose and several other girls surrounded Rebecca and Ana.

"You're so lucky," Rose said to Ana. "You've only been in school for two days, and now you're going to sing at the assembly!"

Ana clasped her hands together nervously. "I hope I can learn fastly," she said. She turned and smiled warmly at Rebecca. "But I not worry. My cousin will teach me."

Ana went off to try jumping rope with some of the girls, but Rebecca headed over to Lucy and Sarah. "I didn't ask Miss Maloney to let Ana sing," Rebecca explained. "It's not my fault."

"It's still not fair," Lucy said firmly. "She can barely speak English. How can she learn the song?"

"If she ruins the performance, the whole school will be laughing at us," Sarah added. "You're going to have to do a good job teaching her the song, or it will be your fault."

Rebecca's stomach tightened into a knot.

Rebecca was quiet on the way home, while Ana bubbled over with excitement. As they headed up the front stoop, Rebecca saw Mr. Rossi's curtains flap closed. Was he spying to see if Ana and her family had moved yet?

Ana raced up the steps and, in a stream of Yiddish, happily told Aunt Fannie and Mama about the assembly.

"Mazel tov! Congratulations!" said Aunt Fannie. She hugged Ana. "I'm so glad you are happy in American school."

"We'd better practice," Rebecca said, "if you're going to learn the song." She took two apples from the bowl on the table. "Come on, Ana, I'll take you to the best place in the building." Ana followed Rebecca up the hall stairs, past Bubbie and Grandpa's apartment, all the way to the top of the stairway. Rebecca pushed open a rickety wooden door, and the girls stepped out onto the flat rooftop. A soft ruffling of feathers and cooing sounds greeted them.

"Birds!" Ana exclaimed, rushing to the wire cages stacked along one side of the roof.

"They're pigeons," Rebecca said. "They're Mr. Rossi's, but I like to come up and look at them. I think they know me." She bit off a piece of her apple and held it up to a cage. A tan bird with black spots eagerly pecked at it. Rebecca reached in two fingers and gently stroked its feathers.

"It's hard to imagine grouchy Mr. Rossi keeping birds,

isn't it," Rebecca said as the girls fed them pieces of apple.

Ana nodded. When her apple was gone, she took the sheet music from Rebecca. "I'm so glad we will sing together at assembly," Ana said. "We will be two songbirds." She began to sing.

Rebecca listened as Ana's melodic notes rose above the cooing of the pigeons. Ana had a pretty voice. If she could learn to say the words properly, she might make a good singing partner. If not, the performance would be ruined.

Carefully, Rebecca had her cousin repeat the words. "It's not 'grend,'" she explained patiently, "but 'grand.' Listen to the a-a-a sound." Ana repeated the word until she got it right. Then they went on to the word "flag," and the same problem came back.

"No, no, no," Rebecca said, feeling exasperated. "It's fl-a-a-a-g, not fl-eh-g." Over and over, they sang the verses, but Ana either forgot the words or mispronounced them.

If Ana can't sing the song properly, Rebecca thought, *I'll be humiliated. And what's worse, my class will be embarrassed in front of the entire school.*

The wooden door creaked open, and Victor and Michael stepped out onto the roof.

"Beckie, Mama wants you girls to set the table," Victor said. "She's determined to get all thirteen of us in the parlor for dinner. Grandpa's bringing down more chairs."

"What have you heard about Josef?" Ana asked her brother, speaking in Yiddish.

Michael slouched against the wall. "Josef is still sick with a fever from his infected leg," he answered. "Doctors are treating him at the Ellis Island infirmary, but they don't know if his leg will heal." He touched Ana's shoulder, and Rebecca saw that his hand was shaking. "If Josef loses his leg, he will have to go back to Russia."

"That would be so unfair," Rebecca said angrily. "Why does it matter if someone has an injured leg?"

"Papa says every immigrant must be able to support himself," Victor explained. "A lame person can't work."

"That's ridiculous," Rebecca exclaimed. "Josef is only fifteen. His family will take care of him. Even if he is lame, he could be a lawyer or a bank clerk who sits at a desk all day!"

Victor shrugged. "Papa says it's the law."

"Well, it's a bad law," Rebecca declared.

Michael spoke up. "There's some good news, too. Papa found a job today, cutting cloth for coats."

Rebecca couldn't stop herself. "He's going to work in a sweatshop?" she blurted.

Michael shrugged. "It's only until a better job comes along." He stood a little straighter. "I'm going to work, too. The dairy company needs boys to move the big milk cans from the delivery wagons to the warehouse. Papa told the manager I was fourteen." He flexed his skinny arm. "The cans might be a little heavy, but I will build up my muscles."

"What about school?" Rebecca asked.

"Since Josef isn't here, I must help earn money," Michael said. Then he looked a bit doubtful. "Maybe I can go to school at night—if I'm not too tired."

Why are things going so wrong? Rebecca asked herself. If Josef were sent back to Russia, his family would never see him again. Uncle Jacob had taken a job in a factory, where he would work long hours under terrible conditions. And now Michael had to leave school.

The rooftop door opened, and Mr. Rossi stood glaring at them. He held a pail of birdseed.

"This roof is not a playground. *Shoo!*" he called, as if they were birds who could fly away. Then Mr. Rossi realized exactly who was on the roof.

"You still here?" he asked Michael. "You can't stay any longer. I am telling landlord tomorrow."

"You don't need to tell the landlord anything, Mr. Rossi," Victor said. "My uncle just rented a tenement on Orchard Street. The whole family is going to move next week."

Fear filled Ana's eyes. "Orchard Street?" she echoed. "The place with dark buildings and big noises and—" Her voice broke as she turned to Rebecca. "I don't want to leave," she cried. "You are like sister to me." Rebecca reached out to hug her cousin, but Ana ran from the rooftop, leaving Rebecca and the cooing birds behind her.

"Now," Mr. Rossi said, "the rest of you, off the roof!"

A New Flag Waves

T hat night, Rebecca tried to comfort her cousin, but Ana's tears wouldn't stop. She cried herself to sleep, her handkerchief clutched in her hand.

Rebecca tossed and turned, thinking about Ana moving to Orchard Street. Next week, Ana would go to a different school. Rebecca had expected her cousin to live with her for a long time and be her partner in everything. She remembered the excitement of bargaining with the peddlers, and thought about how much fun it was to dress alike. Just as Ana had said, they were like sisters. Even better—they were like twins.

It was wonderful having Ana with her all the time—at least, it was wonderful until Miss Maloney decided Ana should sing in the assembly. Now Rebecca's stomach felt queasy whenever she thought about the performance. This was one thing she didn't want to do with Ana.

By morning, Rebecca was too tired to even talk, but it hardly mattered. Ana barely said a word all the way to school. Her eyes were puffy, and she seemed ready to cry again at any moment. Rebecca was silent, too, as the class filed into the big auditorium for rehearsal. The students lined up on the stage, facing the empty chairs where the rest of the school would sit in just two days.

"You may read your poems today, since it's just the first practice," Miss Maloney said. "But tomorrow is already Thursday, and you must have them memorized by then. Remember that this assembly is to show our respect for the flag. I expect each of you to recite your poems perfectly and with great feeling. Leo," Miss Maloney called, "you will begin the program by explaining why we have a new flag. Step forward, please."

Leo straightened his tweed jacket and puffed out his chest. "In 1912, America welcomed two new states to the Union," he began.

All through rehearsal Rebecca fidgeted, anxiously awaiting her moment onstage. She knew the song perfectly now. If only Ana would sing without any mistakes!

When all the other students had recited their pieces, Rebecca and Ana moved to the front of the stage. Miss Maloney sat down at the piano, spreading her silky black skirt across the piano stool. She opened the sheet music and played the opening notes. The girls began to sing.

Ana's rich voice sounded even prettier with the piano to accompany her. Rebecca tried to close her ears to her cousin's accent. Although Rebecca had drilled her repeatedly, Ana just couldn't seem to pronounce a short "a" sound. She said "fleg" instead of "flag" and "lend" instead of "land." As Rebecca boomed out the last two lines, she suddenly realized she was singing alone. Ana had forgotten the words completely! Ana looked at her in panic and then ran from the stage, her footsteps echoing down the hallway. Rebecca stood alone, her voice trailing off. Her classmates groaned.

"Let's be polite, children," Miss Maloney scolded them. "Rebecca and Ana are still learning the song."

Me? thought Rebecca. *Why, I know the song perfectly. It's Ana who's spoiling it!*

When the rehearsal was over, Rebecca found Ana alone in the classroom. As the other students filed in, Ana murmured, "I practice harder." She looked up at Rebecca. "You will help?"

Rebecca couldn't even answer. She took her pencil to the pencil sharpener, feeling the other students' eyes on her as she walked across the room.

Sarah cornered her. "Ana barely knows the words, and when she does, she can't even say them in proper English."

"Shhh," Rebecca said. "She might hear you." She turned the pencil sharpener handle harder until the lead point was as sharp as a needle. "What can I do?" she demanded in a loud whisper. "I'm not the one making the mistakes!"

"Well, she's *your* cousin," Sarah said. She twisted a fold of her dress anxiously. "Please don't let her ruin the assembly. Our class will be the laughingstock of the school!" She put her hand on Rebecca's shoulder. "Why don't you just tell her she can't sing with you?"

Gertie chimed in from her seat nearby. "That would solve the whole problem. I'm sure Miss Maloney would agree. She said everything has to be perfect to show our respect for the flag."

Rebecca walked slowly back to her desk. Everyone was counting on her. *It will be my fault if the assembly is ruined,* she thought. Should she tell her cousin not to sing?

Then Rebecca thought of something else. Perhaps Ana didn't *want* to sing anymore. Now that she saw how difficult it was, she might be relieved if she didn't have to practice the words and worry about saying them perfectly. Next week, she would be going to a different school anyway, so maybe being part of the assembly didn't matter to her now.

When the class was dismissed for lunch, Ana stayed at her desk, hunched over the sheet music. Rebecca dawdled at the closet when she got her lunch box. *Maybe this is the time to tell Ana not to sing,* she thought. Then she heard her cousin's voice floating softly across the room. "You're grend old fleg and high-flyink fleg . . ." Rebecca grabbed her lunch box and hurried out to find Rose.

"Where's *En*na?" Otto Geller teased as Rebecca rushed by. "Is she looking at the *fleg*?"

Rebecca's face flushed with anger. She turned her back on Otto and marched over to join Rose.

"Everyone thinks it will be my fault if Ana ruins the assembly," Rebecca said to Rose as she sat down beside her.

Rose unwrapped a *knish* and took a bite of the potato-filled pastry. "What do *you* think?" she asked.

"I've tried to teach her the song, but there isn't enough time," Rebecca replied. "I think Ana might make a lot of mistakes."

"She might," Rose agreed. "It's very hard to learn English, and Ana's only been here a few days."

"If the assembly is ruined because of Ana, the whole class will be disappointed, including Miss Maloney. And I'll be the one who let them down. I bet no one will ever speak to me again."

Rose looked doubtful. "How long do you really think they'll remember?"

"Probably forever," said Rebecca. She still remembered her humiliation when Miss Maloney made her wear the dunce cap. But Rebecca suddenly realized that she hadn't thought about the dunce cap at all since that day. And none of her classmates had said a word about the dunce cap, not even Leo.

Rebecca nibbled at her lunch. "Sarah thinks I should tell Ana she can't sing with me. Maybe she's right. I'm sure Ana's worried about spoiling the song," Rebecca pointed out. "She must be worried, or she wouldn't have run off the stage this morning when she forgot the words. She might be relieved if I tell her not to sing."

"Maybe." Rose shrugged. "How would you feel if you were Ana?"

"Well, I know I wouldn't want to be embarrassed in front of the whole school," said Rebecca.

Miss Maloney rang the bell, and Rebecca followed Rose back to class. She had eaten only a few bites, but she didn't feel hungry at all.

Rose's question burned in her head for the rest of the day. *How would you feel?* Rebecca already knew how she'd feel if Ana did sing and made mistakes. But how would Ana feel if Rebecca kept her out of the assembly?

⧉⊙⧉

As soon as she opened her eyes Friday morning, Rebecca felt a nervous flutter in the pit of her stomach. Yesterday's rehearsal had gone no better. Ana either forgot the words or pronounced them wrong. Miss Maloney had looked at the girls with pursed lips and hadn't said a word. Rebecca couldn't bear to let everyone down, especially her teacher.

Now the assembly was starting in just a few hours. If

she was going to tell Ana not to sing, she had to do it soon. But Ana had already gone into the kitchen for breakfast. Quickly, Rebecca began getting dressed.

Rose's question pricked at her. *How would you feel if you were Ana?*

Well, how *would* she feel? Rebecca looked in the mirror and pictured Ana saying to her, "Your voice not so pretty. I not want you to sing with me." Abruptly, Rebecca sat down hard on the bed as a hot wave of terrible feelings washed over her. She blinked, and then again she imagined it, Ana telling her not to sing. Her chest burned with hurt and humiliation. The feeling was far, far worse than the embarrassment she had felt onstage when Ana forgot the words. Rebecca swallowed. Her mouth felt dry. She knew she would never forget it if Ana were to push her out of the assembly.

Mama beamed at the girls over breakfast. "It's so nice to see you matching every day." Rebecca managed a thin smile, but Ana didn't even look up.

Aunt Fannie handed each girl a small American flag. "We got these at Immigration when we came," she said. "Maybe they will bring you luck this morning when you sing."

Rebecca thanked her aunt politely and gave her flag a limp wave. Ana simply dropped hers into her pocket.

Bubbie came in with a plate of dark rolls, and Grandpa poked his head in the door. "I'll handle the store myself this morning," he said to Papa. "I hope everything goes well with Josef."

Papa, Aunt Fannie, and Uncle Jacob were going to Ellis Island once again. Josef's fever had broken, and the Hebrew Immigrant Aid Society had arranged for the family to meet with immigration officials. Rebecca's aunt had replaced her kerchief with one of Mama's hats, and Uncle Jacob had trimmed his beard neatly.

Suddenly Aunt Fannie sank into a chair. "What if the immigration men say Josef cannot stay?" she worried.

It would be wrong to force Josef to leave America just because his leg wasn't perfect, Rebecca felt certain. Now she realized it would also be wrong to force Ana out of the assembly just because her English wasn't perfect. Maybe Rebecca and her classmates would be embarrassed if the song was a flop, but in just a few days, nobody would remember or care. Yet if she told Ana not to sing . . .

Rebecca ran to the bedroom and grabbed her doll from the pillow. *Please bring good luck today*, she whispered as she slipped Beckie into her pocket.

As the girls walked to school, Ana looked directly at Rebecca. "Don't worry," she said. "I not sing today and ruin assembly."

Rebecca stopped short. "What do you mean? I didn't say anything about your singing." A shiver of shame crept up her neck. How could Ana have known what she had been thinking?

"You don't have to say anything to me," Ana said softly. "I hear you and Sarah and Lucy talking. You think I am dunce?"

Rebecca's heart sank. "I *was* worried about the performance," she admitted, "but now—now I *do* want you to sing with me, Ana. Honest."

"Now is too late," Ana said. "I tried hard, but I know things not always fair. Just like with Josef." She rushed ahead, leaving Rebecca to walk the rest of the way alone.

At school, Rebecca tried to talk to Ana as they filed into the auditorium. "We're two songbirds—remember?" But Ana turned away.

The class crowded together near the stage steps as Miss Maloney went to turn on the stage lights. Sarah pulled Rebecca aside.

"Did you tell her?" she whispered. Rebecca shook her head. Sarah didn't make a sound, but her mouth moved to form the words "Oh, no!"

Rebecca turned away, fighting back tears. Now *everyone* was unhappy with her. The performance hadn't even begun, and already she had ruined everything.

"Are we ready?" Miss Maloney said cheerily. "Line up, boys and girls."

As the students formed a line, Rebecca gazed at the high ceiling and the dark paneled walls. Painted in gold lettering along the top of the walls were the names of famous American presidents: George Washington, Thomas Jefferson, Abraham Lincoln. She felt as if they were ready to welcome the new flag, too. But was she?

Rebecca took a deep breath and walked over to Ana. Her cousin had not joined the line of classmates waiting to step onto the stage. Rebecca pulled her Russian doll from her pocket. "You take Beckie," she said, handing the doll to Ana. "She brought me good luck in the audition, and now she'll bring us both good luck in the assembly."

Ana held the little doll close. "Do you really think I should sing, Rebecca?" she asked softly.

"Of course you should," Rebecca assured her. "You have the prettiest voice in the class. Now come on, let's get in line!"

Feet shuffled and chairs creaked while the audience took their seats. Then silence fell as Miss Maloney stepped to the front of the stage and welcomed the school to the assembly.

Leo began his opening speech, but Rebecca's heart was beating so loudly that she barely heard him. She looked out at the sea of upturned faces and drew in a shaky breath. There were so many people, all listening in complete silence. Would they notice every mistake? As her classmates recited their poems, Rebecca's hands began to tremble. It was almost time for her and Ana to sing.

At last, Miss Maloney played the lively opening notes on the piano, and the girls stepped forward. Together, they began the bouncy tune. Rebecca tried to smile and concentrate on her own singing. She barely noticed her cousin's accent and hoped the audience didn't notice it either. Ana's strong voice lifted Rebecca's, and Rebecca's clear words carried Ana's. When they came to the last verse, Rebecca realized that the audience was clapping in rhythm and the assembly seemed alive with enthusiasm. They had nearly made it to the end.

As the piano sounded its final chord, Ana suddenly pulled the small American flag from her pocket and waved it high. Surprised, Rebecca quickly did the same. The entire school cheered and applauded.

Then the lights dimmed, and a bright light shone on the new flag that hung from a pole at the side of the stage. Its rich colors stood out in the darkened hall. The audience rose, and everyone placed their right hands over their hearts and recited the Pledge of Allegiance. But Rebecca's ears were still ringing with the sound of applause. She and

Ana had done it. They had sung for the whole school, and everything had been all right. Ana's accent hadn't mattered at all. And now Miss Maloney was beaming proudly as the principal came onstage and shook her hand. The assembly was a success.

Rebecca thought she saw tears brimming in Ana's eyes, but her cousin's face was lit up with happiness. Rebecca squeezed Ana's hand, and Ana squeezed back.

"Why did you wave your flag?" Rebecca whispered.

"I am feeling *patriotic*," Ana said, motioning to the back of the audience. "Look!"

Rebecca peered through the dim light and saw a row of people standing near the wall. She could see her mother, her father, Uncle Jacob, and Aunt Fannie—and beside them was a tall, lanky boy with a thickly bandaged leg leaning on a wooden crutch. Rebecca waved her flag in his direction, and from his pocket, Josef pulled an identical flag and waved it high in the air.

✎❧ GLOSSARY ❧✎

Amerikanka (ah-mair-ee-KONG-kah)—the Russian way to say American

bar mitzvah (bar MITS-vah)—the ceremony honoring a boy's first reading of the Hebrew Bible before the congregation, and also the boy himself; Hebrew for "son of the commandment"

bubbie (BUH-bee)—the Yiddish word for grandmother

hallah (HAH-lah; often spelled "challah")—a Hebrew word for a rich white bread made with eggs and usually braided

knish (kuh-NISH)—in Yiddish, a food made of dough stuffed with a filling, such as potato, then baked or fried

kopek (KOH-pek)—a small Russian coin, similar to a penny

mazel tov (MAH-zl tof)—Hebrew for congratulations!

mitzvah (MITS-vah)—a good deed, and also the duty to perform acts of kindness; Hebrew for "commandment"

nudge (nooj; same vowel sound as in "wood")—in Yiddish, a pushy pest

oy vey (oy VAY)—a Yiddish exclamation meaning oh dear!

pushke (PUSH-kee)—in Yiddish, a small can or box used to collect money for charity

samovar (SAM-oh-var)—a Russian urn used to heat water for tea

schlepping (SHLEP-ing)—Yiddish for hauling or lugging

scusi (SKOO-zee)—Excuse me in Italian

Shabbos (SHAH-bes)—Yiddish for Sabbath, the day of rest

shah (shah)—the Yiddish way to say shush!

trousseau (troo-SOH)—the household goods that a bride brings to her marriage; originally a French word

tsar (zar; often spelled "czar")—the Russian word for emperor

zayda (ZAY-dah)—the Yiddish word for grandfather

Inside
Rebecca's World

When Rebecca was growing up, thousands of immigrants were coming to America each year to make new lives. Cities often had entire neighborhoods settled by people from one country. Most immigrants entered the United States at New York City's Ellis Island, as Ana's family did. The largest city in America, New York, had millions of Jewish immigrants from Russia and other countries.

In 1914, the Russian Empire was ruled by the powerful Tsar Nicholas II. The tsar did not regard his Jewish subjects as real Russians, because the Jews practiced a different religion and spoke a different language: Yiddish. Jews were barred from most jobs and could not own land or

Hester Street in New York City, where many immigrants lived

travel freely. Even worse, Russian soldiers and villagers sometimes led *pogroms*, or violent attacks on Jews. They broke into Jewish homes, shops, and temples, looting and burning—and often killing, too. They did this out of *prejudice*, the belief that people who are different are bad.

Tsar Nicholas II

Jews like Rebecca's and Ana's parents decided to move to countries where their families could lead better lives. Between 1880 and 1914, two million Jews left Russia and Eastern Europe and came to the United States.

These families became homeless after their homes were ransacked by Russian soldiers.

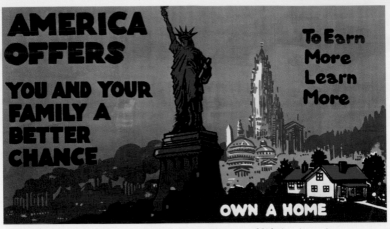

AMERICA OFFERS YOU AND YOUR FAMILY A BETTER CHANCE

To Earn More Learn More

OWN A HOME

A poster advertising the advantages of life in America

Immigrants brought the traditions of their old countries to America, but they adapted to new ways, too. Most Jewish immigrants spoke Yiddish, like Rebecca's grandparents, but they learned English. On Friday evenings, Jewish families welcomed the Sabbath with candles and prayers. The Sabbath, which lasted until sundown on Saturday, was supposed to be a day of rest, but like Rebecca's father, many Jews had to work on Saturday to feed their families. The immigrants who followed Jewish traditions more strictly, like Bubbie and Grandpa, often disapproved of those who did not. This conflict between old ways and new ways is one that many immigrants face when they move to a new country.

At a Sabbath dinner, special blessings are said over the candles, the hallah loaves, and the cup of wine.

Whether they had been in the United States for generations or were newcomers, most Americans enjoyed attending vaudeville shows, which had a variety of song and dance acts, comedians, magicians, and even animal acts. Many

The Marx Brothers were vaudeville comedians before becoming comedy movie stars.

movie actors got their start in vaudeville, just like Mama's cousin Max did. By 1914, vaudeville theaters were also showing movies. Especially popular were serials, such as *The Perils of Pauline*, which showed a new episode every week.

The actress Pearl White, who played Pauline

A 1914 movie poster

Before the main feature, theaters would show a newsreel, a short film about current events. People were eager to see newsreels about the First World War, which had just broken out in Europe. Although the United States had not yet entered the war, Americans were keenly interested in it. Jews were especially concerned about their relatives back in Russia and raised as much money as they could to help them.

After the war started, it became much more difficult to leave Europe. In contrast to the millions of immigrants who had come in the previous years, only a few more people were able to get out of Russia, as Ana's family did, and come to safety in America.

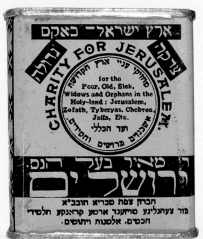

*Every Jewish family had a **pushke**, or charity box, to collect money for Jews in need.*

Lights, Camera, Rebecca!

"I've got a great idea," Rebecca said. "Let's act out a movie about a worker in a coat factory. Movies have happy endings, so in our movie everyone will get a raise."

Ana perked up. "That sounds good! And since I know what the factories are like, I could play the boss." Ana took one of her father's hats from a nail on the wall and plopped it on her head. "I'll be Mr. Simon. He's the boss." She draped her mother's shawl around Rebecca's shoulders and sat her at a small table in the tiny parlor. "You can be a poor stitcher who's just come to America."

"Okay," Rebecca said. She bent over the table as if she were leaning over a sewing machine.

"You really have to slump over," Ana directed. "Look as if you're too tired and hot to even push the fabric through."

Rebecca followed Ana's instructions, imagining that her shoulders ached from bending over the machine.

"Faster! Faster!" Ana ordered. "You're too slow."

Rebecca really was sweating. She reached up and wiped the perspiration from her forehead.

"Aha!" Ana shouted, pointing an accusing finger. "You are not allowed to stop your machine without my permission!" Ana pretended to pull out a notebook and write in it. "You will lose one hour of pay this week."

Rebecca clasped her hands together. "Please, Mr. Simon," she begged, "Don't take any money from my pay. If I can't pay the rent, the landlord will throw us out on the street!"

"And no talking!" Ana gave a mean smile. "I'll be kind and only take out a nickel for talking instead of working."

"What?" Rebecca was indignant. "How can you punish me for nothing? If you don't treat the workers fairly, we will walk out of this factory and go on strike."

Ana sneered. "Go ahead and strike. There are plenty more workers coming off the boat who will take this job in a minute." She pointed to the door. "You do what I tell you, or you're fired."

Rebecca's heart was beating fast. No matter what she said, Ana seemed to get the better of her. "Why are you being so mean, Ana?" she sputtered. "In our movie, the workers are supposed to get a raise. You're not playing fair!"

Ana folded her arms across her chest. "I'm not Ana—I'm Mr. Simon. That means I can do whatever I want, and you have to go along with it."

Anger rose in Rebecca's chest. She couldn't do anything without being punished. The movie wasn't fun anymore.

"CUT!" Rebecca yelled, pulling off the shawl. "Why are you doing this, Ana?"

"I'm acting in a movie, just like you said," Ana replied. "I'm being a factory boss."

"Well, you don't have to be so mean," Rebecca protested. "And so unfair."

a Nez Perce girl who loves daring
adventures on horseback

a Jewish girl with a secret
ambition to be an actress

who joins the war effort
when Hawaii is attacked

whose big ideas get her into
trouble—but also save the day

who finds the strength to lift
her voice for those who can't

who fights for the right to play
on the boys' basketball team